CAPTIVATED BY THE ENIGMATIC TYCOON

BY
BELLA BUCANNON

MILLS & BOON

First Published in Great Britain 2017
By Mills & Boon, an imprint of HarperCollins*Publishers*
1 London Bridge Street, London, SE1 9GF

© 2017 Harriet Nichola Jarvis

ISBN: 978-0-263-06954-9

Our policy is to use papers that are natural, renewable and recyclable
products and made from wood grown in sustainable forests. The logging
and manufacturing processes conform to the legal environmental
regulations of the country of origin.

Printed and bound in Great Britain
by CPI Antony Rowe, Chippenham, Wiltshire

Bella Bucannon lives in a quiet northern suburb of Adelaide with her soulmate husband, who loves and supports her in any endeavour. She enjoys walking, dining out and travelling. Bus tours or cruising with days at sea to relax, plot and write are top of her list. Apart from category romance she also writes very short stories and poems for a local writing group. Bella believes joining RWA and SARA early in her writing journey was a major factor in her achievements.

Books by Bella Bucannon

Mills & Boon Romance

Bound by the Unborn Baby
A Bride for the Brooding Boss

Visit the Author Profile page at millsandboon.co.uk.

To my own special hero,
who understands my struggle with routine
and being organised.

To Flo and Victoria
for their support, advice and guidance.

And to everyone who knows I am a hoarder
and couldn't believe I understand decluttering.

CHAPTER ONE

JACK RANDELL GRINNED at the sound of Strauss, his Aunt Mel's favourite composer, as he reached the back door. Hopefully this meant her feisty spirit was resurfacing as she'd rarely listened to any music she could dance to since the accident three months ago.

Although she was technically his great-aunt, he could never envision her as being that extra generation older. She and Bob had given him unconditional support during his teenage years when understanding between him and his parents had seemed irretrievable. This house had become his sanctuary, still was even at the age of twenty-eight.

His spirits lifted in anticipation that she'd also begun baking again, and that the kitchen would be filled with mouth-watering aromas. He automatically inhaled as he stepped across the threshold.

No tempting smells and no sound of human activity. He wasn't surprised at the lack of heating; Mel rarely turned it on until the sun began to set. While he'd been visiting his parents in Brisbane, he'd thought July's bitterly cold days in Adelaide might have changed her mind. Another reason to believe she was active again and didn't need it.

After glancing into the kitchen, disappointingly neat and clean, he was about to call out when he heard a scraping sound from the family room on his right. He walked in and stopped, breath caught in his throat and heart skipping intermittent beats.

An enticingly filled-out pair of denim jeans occupied the space in front of the heavy coffee table now placed in the far corner. Definitely not Mel, who declared denim was for the young. *His* tightened as the pleasing form leaned in further, angling past the bookcase that had been pushed almost to the table, partly blocking the window.

He heard a triumphant *huff*, followed by a pained, 'Ow.' The taut bottom jiggled, and he became decidedly uncomfortable. Mesmerised and immobilised, he watched as the wriggling continued towards him.

A long-sleeved navy woollen jumper appeared, followed by a cap of cropped black hair. The woman snaked onto her haunches, holding up a small object. Her light harmonious laugh rippled through him as she rubbed a spot on the top of her head.

'Got you. I'll sew you back on later.'

'Cassie, coffee time. I'll… Jack, I didn't expect this early surprise!'

Fixated on the figure in front of him, Jack didn't react to his aunt's voice. He was spellbound as the head spun, dark hair flew and a hand hit the floor to prevent toppling over. Scrambling to her feet, she twisted towards him and he found himself fighting for air again.

Walnut-coloured eyes framed by long black lashes widened as a delightful pink hue tinted her cheeks. Natural red, not quite symmetrical lips parted as she sucked in a deep breath and glared at him as if he'd been the cause of her injury.

Holding her gaze, he suddenly jerked back as Mel's face loomed into his vision, eyebrows raised, perceptive smile in place. A great improvement since he'd said goodbye sixteen days ago.

'Remember me?'

He wrapped her in a bear hug and kissed her cheek, thankful she'd regained her normal happy disposition.

'Great timing as always. Coffee in the lounge, and you can tell me how your parents are. Oh, by the way, this is Cassie Clarkson. Cassie, my great-nephew, Jack Randell.'

She walked out with a slight hint of a limp, paying no heed to his dropped jaw. Who the hell was Cassie Clarkson, and what was she doing here when Mel had family who'd willingly come any time she needed help? Had she provided references for whatever she did, and had they been checked?

Hadn't his aunt learnt from previous attempts to cheat her, two of them by so-called friends? An older woman on her own was considered an easy target by unscrupulous people. Even he had been duped by an attractive friend of his sister. He'd lost unpaid rent, plus his own time getting the damaged property fit to let again.

The young woman who was pinning whatever she'd picked up onto a coat hanging on a clothes rack—he now became aware of it, plus two by the window—was delightfully curved and a perfect height to nestle her head cosily on his shoulder.

Which he really should not be imagining when he had no idea who, why or what as far as she was concerned. Good looks and toned bodies might attract but they could also mask a desire for the lifestyle and prestige marrying into a wealthy family offered. Hard lessons learnt weren't easily forgotten.

Ignoring the acceleration of his pulse and the warmth spreading through his body despite the cool air, he stepped forward. She looked up, and he had a hankering for warm Christmas brandy heated by the glow in her eyes. Instantly tempered by his self-imposed wariness of mere physical attraction. He took another pace and held out his hand.

'Hello, Cassie.'

She wiped hers on her thighs before accepting.

'Dust. Hello, Jack. Mel's mentioned you a few times.'

She kept their touch brief, barely polite, and removed her hand smoothly so she couldn't have felt the *zing* that shot through him. Neither did she sound as impressed as he'd like her to be, though there was no reason for him to care. Or for his fingers to involuntarily try to hold on. He definitely liked the slightly rough edge to her voice.

'And you don't approve. Any particular reason?'

She laughed again, triggering the same response. 'I never make hasty judgements. I admire the way she portrays you, your siblings and cousins as paragons of virtue; I'm just convinced she's oblivious to your faults.'

He suspected she was baiting him, didn't rise. 'She brings out the best in us. Who exactly are you and what are you doing here?'

'I'm a declutterer.'

'A what?'

Cassie wasn't fazed by his bewilderment, and quite liked the baffled expression on his handsome rugged face. Payback for not letting her know he was observing her ungainly exit from under the table. She'd caught her breath as they'd made contact and wondered if he'd felt the same electrical spark that zapped up her arm.

'I help people sort out and downsize their belongings.'

'Mel's not a hoarder.' Quick and sharp.

'No, she's not, and she's expecting us for coffee.'

She walked past him and went to the kitchen to wash her hands. The tingle on her nape told her he'd followed. She dismissed it, refusing to gush over cowboy hero features and eyes the colour of buffalo grass after spring rain. Or to surrender to the urge to finger comb his ruffled light brown hair. Even if his voice was deep and smooth like the old-time crooners on her mum's CDs.

'So she's hired you. Why keep it quiet?'

His sharp tone irked. Counting to fourteen before turning rather than the universal ten was her safety valve. Failing to get any employer's relative onside could backfire on her.

She enjoyed her work and satisfied customers spread the word, ensuring she rarely had to advertise for clients. He was the first of Mel's relations she'd met, though a niece had visited prior to her arrival this morning, and there'd been a few phone calls.

At her interview, Mel had explained her family regularly checked up on her since she'd insisted she no longer needed a live-in carer. Her hairline fracture had healed with minimal after-effects, and she took care moving around. She still slept in a made-up room downstairs and never went to the second storey when alone.

Today, as they'd worked, she'd chatted about the younger generation, and the way they fussed over her. Cassie's heart had clenched at the thought of having numerous relatives who cared.

Running her hand over her hair, she turned to find Jack almost within touching distance.

If one desired physical contact. Which she did not.

Legs apart, hands tucked into rear pockets and eyes narrowed with suspicion, he appeared to be spoiling for a confrontation.

She met his unblinking stare with confidence, regarding the ripples in her stomach as natural under the circumstances. Showing him she wouldn't be intimidated, she began a slow scroll down his face, noting the high forehead, the wide generous mouth and the strong stubbled jaw. Sculpted biceps and pecs were clearly defined under a fawn work shirt, unbuttoned at the neck and folded at the wrists, revealing tufts of fine brown hair.

Unfortunately, it was *her* pulse quickening and *her* temperature rising as her gaze slid over firm blue denim-clad thighs and past long legs to black tradies' boots. Keeping tight control on the speed, she made the journey up to a gratifying flush and a very masculine scowl.

'I wasn't aware she hadn't told you.' She heard the hitch

in her voice, hoped her features didn't betray her reaction. 'If you'll excuse me, I'll see you in the lounge in a few minutes.'

She walked towards the door, head held high, shoulders rigid.

He moved aside. 'It will be my pleasure.' A tone or two deeper than his last remark, with a definite hint of cynicism.

Upstairs, in the bedroom Mel had invited her to use, she slumped against the closed door, shaken by the encounter with her employer's handyman nephew. The guy wouldn't be out of place on the pages of the celebrity magazines Narelle, her best friend, avidly studied. She could imagine those full, firm lips...*no!* She would not.

Cassie had escaped from him to gather her thoughts, and wasn't sure she'd succeeded even after brushing her hair until it shone. Not for him, she told herself as she went downstairs. Being neat and tidy was a matter of pride.

Her career choice had been a natural progression after assisting the woman she'd called Mum all her life help different friends prepare for the move into retirement villages or homes. At first she'd been fascinated by the variety of, to her teenage eyes, useless items, some not even decorative. There were always old postcards and souvenirs, hardly used presents, and so many photographs in albums, boxes and drawers.

Talking to these people at this crucial moment in their lives, she'd empathised with their anxieties and their pain at having to let go of items that defined their lives. Growing up with no relatives except Mum, she'd found the differences in family interactions intriguing. She'd also discovered she had a talent for sensing the emotional reasons behind the spoken need to cling to certain pieces. The appeal of working in the same building every day, no matter what the job, had diminished in comparison.

* * *

Jack's baritone was audible as Cassie approached the lounge room door, though the actual words were indistinguishable. Their combined laughter triggered a yearning for the closeness she'd shared for twenty-three years with Julie, her maternal aunt, to her, now and for ever, Mum.

At two days old, her birth mother had brought her to Julie then left for America. She'd made spasmodic short visits while Cassie was very young and occasional telephone calls after. There'd been no contact for fifteen years.

The cancer that had taken Mum four years ago had been short and aggressive, but thankfully there was no heart-wrenching guilt for missed opportunities. Every memory was precious, any reminder, however painful, evoked grateful thanks for the time they'd had.

Hearing Jack's voice again, she closed her eyes, pressed her open hands to her lips and breathed in and out twice. Channelling her inner strength, she walked in.

Jack's expression was inscrutable though his lips curled a little as their eyes met. He'd taken the huge armchair in the corner, body at ease, legs stretched out. She'd tried it when they'd had morning tea, felt lost in its size and preferred a corner of the family-sized sofa. Sam, Mel's medium-size, scruffy mixed breed dog, was curled up on the rug in front of him.

'Jack's been enjoying the Queensland sunshine,' Mel explained as she poured a cup of coffee and handed it to Cassie. 'He makes it sound very tempting.'

His velvet tongue would tempt the devil into a trip to the Arctic. Cassie bent to select a chocolate biscuit from the long, low table then sat, arching against the big comfortable cushion. Who needed pricy gyms when they bent, stretched and lifted all day? She worked hard and slept soundly.

'He's a little testy because I hired you without consulting the family first, Cassie. As if I can't decide for myself.'

'Not what I said, Aunt Mel,' he interrupted, eyebrow quirking. 'I asked why you've hired someone when you'd get all the help you need from us.'

Being fit and healthy, he wouldn't understand his aunt's wish to regain independence after relying on her extended family's care and attention for so long. This was a major step in her rehabilitation.

'And I appreciate it, dear.' Her employer grinned at Cassie. 'I can also detect censure. It's the *Aunt* Mel. If he's really cross I become *Great-Aunt Melanie*.'

Her affection was so clear Cassie smiled then swung in Jack's direction as he burst out laughing. It was a rich crackly sound, generating an image of a campfire in the Outback. Bizarre, as she'd never had the experience.

'Guess who I learnt that from. I knew I was in big trouble whenever you called me Jackson Randell in that quiet, resolute tone guaranteed to have any of us kids confessing every misdemeanour.'

'*Jackson?*' Never ever would Cassie have visualised him with such a distinctive name. All she'd heard and seen—apart from his movie star looks—said regular working guy who'd had normal teenage disputes with his parents. Yet now, as she studied him, she became aware of an innate assurance that tested her ever-present caution. Evidence of well-to-do family and a private education.

'Only ever used on official documents or by aggrieved mother and aunts.' His eyes sobered, locked with hers. Straightening up, he put his coffee mug down and leant his elbows on the chair arms. Sam crept forward, laying his head on Jack's boot.

'Mel insisted you be present when she explained what's going on, Cassie.'

Although he pronounced it like everyone else, his timbre as he said her name triggered tingles across her skin.

She detected a slight undertone, a hint of warning and was glad Mel spoke first, causing him to turn her way.

'I've had a lot of time to think lately about life, and being dependent on people, Jack. It's made me realise I'm not as resilient as I've always believed. I need to get my home and affairs in order before I become doddery and senile.'

Jack shook his head and chuckled, and the image of a wide plain and starlit sky flared again.

'Mel Frampton, you're one of the brightest, sanest people I know, and I'm grateful to be part of the same gene pool. I also have every intention of leading you onto the dance floor at your centenary celebration.'

'It's a date. Right now, not being game to access the top floor without help is frustrating. I decided to begin with a cull of my clothes and shoes. Apart from my bedroom walk-in, I have two wardrobes full of garments, most of which no longer fit.'

'You were never overweight.' Jack's forceful exclamation surprised both women.

'No, but it's crept on over the years. Not good for an inactive middle-aged woman. Eating more salads and limited baking means I've lost some. Now it's time to get rid of anything that doesn't suit me or fit comfortably. My accident was a reality check.'

'Okay, it doesn't…'

'Cassie, you explain how it works.'

Gee, thanks, Mel. Now I have to confront him and pretend I'm not affected by his piercing green eyes.

The owner of those disturbing eyes shifted in his chair, aligning his body to hers, his posture challenging. He flexed the fingers of his left hand on his thigh. Convincing his sceptical mind that her employment was the better option required tactful honesty.

It wasn't unusual to have relatives question her motives or trustworthiness. There were so many dodgy crooks trying to take advantage of older people, especially women living alone.

Jack Randell in protective mode was going to be tougher than most to placate. He wasn't budging until he'd been fully informed of her role in his aunt's objectives. Cassie's heart warmed at the unmistakable love and concern driving his determination.

'Every situation is different, depending on the needs of my clients. I never try to influence their choices. Satisfied referrals are my main source of employment.'

His body eased and his furrowed brow cleared.

She continued. 'All items are listed on a tablet which stays at the client's home. On completion, they receive a printout and backup on USB then my files are cleared.'

'Completely?' His shirt tightened across his chest as he breathed in and squared his shoulders. It was a very *I'm-the-male-here* action that ought to rankle yet didn't.

She steeled her resolve. Macho didn't impress her but… her practical mind appreciated a man this fit would be handy on many of the assignments she accepted. At least his muscles would; the effect his proximity seemed to have on her might not be so welcome.

'Jackson.' Mel's tone was sharp and every sign of intimidation evaporated.

CHAPTER TWO

JACK SMILED AT his aunt, let out a huff of breath and picked up his coffee, relishing the strong rich flavour. He'd hold his tongue for now and do his own private investigation of Ms Cassie Clarkson later.

He refocused on the alluring stranger with the steady gaze who unsettled his heartbeat and had him speculating how dark her eyes would grow in desire. How many other men had she swayed with her pacifying manner? Not his affair. *Bad choice of word.*

He gave her his full attention as she continued, noting liquid had no effect on her unique voice. Did passion?

Focus, Randell.

'Family contribution and involvement can be emotive, which often leads to controversy. I always recommend nothing is given to charity or thrown away without consultation.'

'We decided the best plan was to bring everything downstairs for me to check,' Mel interjected, and he swung towards her.

'The clothes I want for use will go in the room I'm sleeping in now, and others for keeping can go back to my bedroom. The family will be invited to help themselves from the rest. Now, are you going to play nice or do I ban you until we've finished?'

She wouldn't.

One glance at her beloved, resolute face and he capitulated. Being forbidden to come here was unthinkable, even for a short time. He held both hands up in defeat, his empty mug hanging on one finger.

'Okay, I surrender. Need help with anything? I'm free for the rest of the day.' Though his expertise in women's clothes was more in the line of removing them, not shifting them around.

'I do have a list of minor repairs you can look at. Would you like to stay for dinner?'

'Do you need to ask?' He stood up just as a new symphony came through the speakers set high in two corners. 'It's good to hear Strauss again. I feel a definite urge to waltz you round the furniture right now.'

Mel laughed. 'Give my leg a little longer, and I'll accept.' She rose gracefully to her feet, pride in her voice as she told Cassie, 'I taught all his generation proper ballroom dancing.'

Jack's heart swelled at her lithe movements, belying her age and the trauma she'd been through. He prayed she'd stay as bright and feisty for many years. Seeing Cassie sneak an extra chocolate biscuit as she got to her feet, he raised his eyebrows. She noticed and her eyes sparkled, daring him to comment as she took a bite.

He let his gaze flick over her slender figure then grinned. Dipping his head, he gestured for her to precede him to the door, admiring the delectable view as she did.

He prided himself on his judgement of character, improved through the years of buying and renting properties, and honed by the few instances of being conned. It failed him where Cassie Clarkson was concerned, and he didn't want to dwell too much on the reason. He'd treat her with respect and ignore his attraction, though keeping an eye on her wouldn't be hard to take at all.

Having strangers think he wasn't as affluent as Mel or others suited him fine. He relished the hands-on work he did equally with the intellectual stimulation of the stock market. He enjoyed the easy relationship with the people he

did maintenance jobs for, and disliked the fact it would lose
its informality if they found out he was also their landlord.

Flaunting his initial successes, even to his family, had
seemed conceited so he played it down, not worried if others believed he wasted his potential. He understood how
money influenced people's attitude, having let it rule him
in his teens. Personal ambition had driven him to seek
after-school employment and invest in shares.

He'd soon discovered that for some girls his name and
the prospect of money took priority over the person behind
them. Now wiser, and matured by experience, he wanted
people to admire him because of who he was, and how he
acted, not for the numbers on his tax return.

After discussing the precise, neatly written task list with
Mel, he went to fetch appropriate tools from his vehicle.
On his return, he heard voices from the family room and
glanced in. One of the racks was now almost full, there
were evening gowns on the second, and more clothes lay
on the covered billiard table against the side wall.

He couldn't hear what they said but their mingled laughter tipped the scales in Cassie's favour. Mel was happier
than she'd been since the car accident. He backed away and
went to tighten the hinges on the kitchen cupboard doors,
wishing it were a complicated task to keep his mind from
straying to bold walnut-brown eyes and kissable lips.

Cassie made four trips to one of the spare bedrooms for
classical evening wear that sparked a slight twinge of envy.
She loved the textures, colours and styling of brand names
she recognised from magazines. Her yearly spending on
new clothing was probably less than some of these dresses
or outfits had cost on their own.

During her long meeting with Mel over lunch in the
city, and in less than a day here, she'd gained an impression

of an ever-expanding well-educated, affluent family with skilled professions and good standing in the community.

It was also obvious they were close-knit and devoted. She'd seen the same in many families, though had no idea how it really felt to have multiple relatives. There had always been friends to play and share birthdays with but over time many had changed school or moved away.

Narelle had been a constant friend since her family had moved into the neighbourhood when they were both eleven. Within the first week at high school, they'd formed a group with two boys and another girl, the bonds strong to this day. Their families had always welcomed her in their homes, encouraging her to be part of their everyday lives and never giving her reason to feel like an outsider.

Yet much of the time she'd felt as if she had an internal barrier preventing her from allowing herself to completely become part of it all. It was as if she were an audience member who had wandered up onto the stage and didn't know her lines but enjoyed watching from up close.

At odd moments in her youth, usually late at night, she'd sometimes fantasise about having a real sibling. She had never, before or now, had any interest or curiosity about her birth parents. Not even when she'd lost Mum and felt completely alone for a while—still did on occasion, no matter how much support her friends gave her.

This was the main reason she'd rented out the home she'd inherited and moved in with Brad and Phil three years ago. They were as close to brothers as she'd ever have, and would probably tease her mercilessly if she mentioned that spark when she and Jack shook hands.

He was an enigma, born into the elite class of Adelaide yet he'd chosen a trade for his profession. As she went through the foyer, she could hear him humming in the kitchen. It reminded her of Mel's excitement after he'd phoned earlier to say he'd arrived home late yesterday and would call in today.

'He's been my mainstay since Bob died. Could have joined the family law firm but studied business management instead and passed with honours. I don't know why he chose to work in property repair and maintenance, though he is buying houses that he rents out.'

She'd said the latter as if it were the epitome of success.

'He can be very reticent at times, and I'm not sure how many he has, three, maybe more by now, plus his home at Port Noarlunga. I just wish he'd find someone special and settle down. Casual short-term affairs, even if they end without acrimony, are no substitute for a long, happy marriage. I'm sure that mishap... No, that's in the past.'

As far as Cassie was concerned, any attractive male his age who'd never come near to being engaged or married had to have serious commitment issues. Her own situation didn't count. Being illegitimate, alone and knowing nothing of her paternal heritage made her wary of close relationships.

How could she offer any man all he'd desire in a wife and partner when there was no paternal name on her birth certificate? When she had no family history to offer?

'Sorry I've been so long. A friend wanted my recipe for jam drop biscuits.'

Cassie started, though she was getting used to Mel's voice preceding her into a room. Adjusting the straps of a dress on the rack gave her a moment to refocus. The red silk under her fingers was so fine, she could imagine the luxurious texture against her skin as she swayed or danced. It was every woman's dream, a spectacular gown for a romantic waltz in a special man's arms.

Mel came closer. 'Oh, my goodness, I don't even remember some of these clothes. How did I collect so many?'

'You could hold a garage sale and finance a Pacific

cruise.' Jack's amused voice made Cassie spin round. She'd assumed Mel was alone.

'Don't be flippant, Jack.' His aunt's tone softened her words. 'We donate unwanted goods, not sell them.'

'There are outlets for high quality second-hand fashions,' Cassie told them. 'They'd fetch a higher price than a charity could charge, and you could donate the money. We still have to empty the second wardrobe.'

'Hmm, what do you think, Jack?'

'It's worth checking into. Now, if Cassie will show me which hinges need tightening upstairs, I'll get them done now.'

His smile didn't reach his green eyes and her instinct was to decline. He could easily tell which ones were loose so why ask for her help? She answered with a curt nod.

Knowing he was following did funny things to her usual composed bearing, and she found herself taking the stairs with slow careful steps. Heat from his eyes skittled up and down her spine and the ripple in her belly was like a soft breeze stirring waves on the sea. Long steady breaths didn't quell her escalating heartbeat.

She twisted round at the top, grasping the rarity of being almost eye to eye. He caught her elbow without giving her a chance to speak, and gently propelled her to the bedroom at the far end of the passage.

Shaking free from his tingling hold, she stepped back a few paces and kept her voice low. 'As if you need help. This is like a second home for you.' Even huskier than normal when she'd meant to sound forceful.

He leant on the doorjamb, the rigidity of his muscles negating his casual stance, and gazed at her silently, features composed. This was a man adept at verbal negotiations. His lips curled confidently, and *her* body quivered as if he'd stroked warm fingers across her skin. She instinctively re-ran her mantra in her head.

Stay strong. Keep distance.

'Sounds like you've heard a lot in one day, Cassie Clarkson.'

'It comes with the job. People, especially if they live alone, often open up to someone who's temporary and won't have a lasting connection in their life.'

'You remember what they tell you.'

'I've learnt not to retain the sensitive personal stuff. But I'll never forget your aunt's courage and determination to rebuild her life for the second time. She's inspiring.'

He straightened up and took a pace forward. She sucked in air and held her ground.

'She's vulnerable since she lost Bob, even more so now.'

'How long since…?'

'Three years. Two months after their forty-fifth anniversary.' His Adam's apple bobbed as he swallowed. 'Imagine losing someone after forty-five years, how suddenly the one you care about is no longer there.'

She heard deep pain in the last few words, empathised as hers had hardly eased. Was it Bob or someone else he grieved for?

'She has all of you. That's more than some people have.'

His head jerked up and she averted her eyes.

He's smart, Cassie. Guard what you say. Keep strong and quiet.

'I assume you have references that can be verified.' Blunt, as if he regretted showing emotion.

'Of course.' She held his gaze. She had nothing to hide except her inexplicable responses to him.

His low grunt showed he wasn't quite convinced. 'Do you have them with you? May I see them?' Calmly stated with an *I-won't-be-dissuaded* manner.

'Not unless Mel requests it.' She mimicked his attitude, prepared to be polite, refusing to be bullied.

He frowned and came closer, into her personal space.

'She can be too trusting. I'm betting she hasn't asked for them.'

She smelt clean male sweat with a hint of sandalwood each time she inhaled, fought the instinct to run from the room. Yet not from fear; quite the opposite. She had an irrational urge to edge forward, minimise the gap.

Jack could sense a women's attraction for him, but it didn't mean he'd follow through. Cassie was giving out mixed messages. Her body implied *yes*, her eyes were wary and her voice said *no*. She boldly locked eyes with him— he now discerned a fine gold rim round her dark brown irises, yet at times there were shutters, like a misty blind she lowered at will.

She had spunk, hadn't backed off even though he came near enough to detect the faint aroma of peaches. Sweet. Enticing. He was aware of her in a new, unnerving way and his body responded to her, male to female.

His gut feeling said she had secrets hidden behind solid barriers no one was permitted to breach. She could keep them unless they caused trouble for Mel. His life ran smoothly and his long-term strategy for success was on track. As alluring as she was, he'd never let his guard down, never again let a woman believe she could manipulate him.

Tara had swayed him so many times, with her pouting lips and soft caresses, had been convinced she'd succeed again on the trip to the snowfields nine years ago. With blue eyes misting, she'd denied flirting with the ski instructor, only he'd seen her and anger had flared at her lies. Bitter accusations had ended with him telling her to find some other patsy and flinging himself onto the bed they'd shared, telling her not to wake him if she came back.

She hadn't returned. An impulsive decision to ski alone on an unfamiliar track had ended her life. He couldn't change the past but by keeping rigid control of his temper he had command of his future.

Challenge flared in Cassie's eyes, her lips curled and she tilted her head like a beguiling child. 'Why don't you check with her when you come down?'

The emotive tone in her voice didn't quite match the softer personal one in her eyes. And he wasn't sure which one he'd like to pursue, despite his recent vow. He gestured for her to pass and she did.

Too quick. Too close. Her fingers brushed his arm and a bolt of energy shot through him, like nothing he'd felt in his life. She'd been affected too, though she hid her reaction well. Had she picked up static from moving around a large carpeted house all day? Had to be that.

So touch her again and prove it.

Not a chance he was game to take at the moment.

Cassie wasn't sure how she made it out of the room without buckling to the floor. She huffed out the air captured in her lungs when the electrical charge from his touch short-circuited coherent thought and action. Fleeing to the safety of the family room, she was thankful to be alone.

Once she could dismiss as an anomaly, twice was… Did he pick up static electricity in his work? Didn't tradies' boots counteract that? Logic told her they did, as there'd been no reaction when he'd hugged his aunt.

She didn't want to be logical. She wanted to be safe from any involvement with Jack Randell or any other man of his social status. Conceived during an illicit one-night stand, she knew exactly what she was, and how she'd be regarded by elite society. And how easily a man's declared devotion could evaporate when tested.

Jack's appearance and actions gave the impression of a man working his way up the financial ladder, but he had wealthy connections and he'd probably inherit. Whatever the incentive for his current lifestyle, it would be an easy switch to his family's world of fancy cars and fine dining.

She'd never have the luxury of such a choice—her world was compact sedans and home cooking.

Letting out a light self-deprecating laugh, she walked over to the desk where she'd left her laptop next to Mel's computer and printer. Any spark of attraction he'd felt would dissipate at her lack of encouragement.

He'd have jobs waiting to be done during the day and friends to catch up with at night so he probably wouldn't be around much. On Thursday afternoon she'd give Mel her printouts plus a list of exclusive second-hand fashion boutiques, and drive away. That just left tonight to resist his innate charm.

Her body relaxed as she slow breathed, doing her steadying count to fourteen and repeating her mantra. *Stay strong. Keep distance.* She resumed checking labels and sizes, mystified by a world where haute couture and fashion changes were all-important. Why should someone be judged by the brand or style of the clothes they wore?

Neat comfortable jeans and muted tops or jumpers were her standard uniform. Her casual sneakers, boots or safety footwear were a far cry from the large array of high-heeled shoes she'd seen upstairs. They and others with sturdy low heels would be brought down and sorted for the female family members to view.

CHAPTER THREE

JACK WAS MULLING over his conversation with Cassie when
he found Mel setting the table in the dining room. His heart
lifted at the sight of the flower centrepiece and the crystal
glasses beside each place setting, as they'd always been at
dinner before her accident. A few stupid seconds of driving
inattention to check a text and a teenager's car had veered
towards the kerb. Overcorrecting had sent it slamming into
Mel's daughter's passenger door. And Mel.

The weeks in hospital and drawn-out rehabilitation, with
a broken leg and lacerations on her arm and across the
top of her chest, had taken a toll. Table decorations didn't
sound like much but he thanked whatever gods there were
that she seemed to be embracing the life she'd loved again.

Not being able to drive, stand for long to cook and having to convert the small lounge into a downstairs bedroom
had been hard enough. Being reliant on others for everything when she'd struggled so hard to be independent after
Bob's fatal heart attack had almost broken her spirit.

If having the distraction of Cassie Clarkson here for a
few days was the price to pay for getting his beloved Aunt
Mel back to her old self, so be it.

'Going classy, huh? Do I need to race home and change?'

Mel's smile lit up her face, and her eyes shone. 'I thought
Cassie deserved it. She's a sweet girl, and I like her. What
we're doing is good for me, Jack.'

He walked over and hugged her. 'I wholeheartedly approve of anything that makes you happy, Mel.'

'Even if I take it further?'

He pulled back to see her expression. 'As in?'

'As in asking Cassie for a quote for a full downsize. Not all at once—over a few months, in between her other contracts. That way it won't be so tiring and easier to accept.'

A full house sorting? The first step to moving, selling her home. Life-changing for her, and she wanted his approval. This was a chance to make a small repayment for her and Bob's unconditional support.

'If it's what you want and feel you're ready for, I'm with you one hundred percent. You know you can rely on me, Mel.'

He kissed her cheek and stepped back. 'Do I have time to take Sam for a run before we eat?'

'Twenty minutes.' She patted his cheek as if he were a schoolboy again. 'Go.'

He went.

As he pounded along the footpath his mind churned with Mel's revelation. He'd fallen into the trap of believing that Mel's continuing recovery meant life would one day be as it always had been. Though he'd hoped she'd relent and have someone move in with her for company and safety.

She, Bob and their home had been his lifeline when home trauma threatened to derail his carefully planned objectives. He'd managed to get through the usual rebellious stage of drinking and partying without irreparable damage to his reputation.

He'd refused to study for the degree his father had wanted him to take, or to join one of the Randell established businesses, which had caused deep-seated angst. His dream to build a property empire had only been shared with Bob. During their discussions in the garden workshop, his great-uncle had taught him how to repair and maintain a home and its contents. He'd also instilled Jack with respect for his tools and the knowledge of their care and maintenance.

He and Mel had encouraged him when he'd got his first

after-school job, shelf-stacking at a local supermarket, and celebrated with him after he signed the contract to buy his first rental property. His one small consolation when Bob died was that he'd shared in every success, and had been thrilled when Jack had become a millionaire. Even if it was only on paper or consisting of bricks and mortar.

Thinking of that gentle man caused his heart to ache as if he'd run a marathon. He pushed through the pain. They'd always put his needs first; now it was time for him to man up and do the same for Mel.

Even she didn't know the true extent of his current finances. Having everyone believe he was buying a few properties and earning his daily living in maintenance kept him grounded and his demons at bay. Even then he could never be sure if it was him or the knowledge of his family's assets that attracted women. Tara had made it clear that she'd never date anyone she considered below her social status.

Mel's experiences had further proved that wealth drew frauds and con artists. So many people wanted easy money rather than work for it. Did Cassie? Was she wary of him as Mel's protector or as a man? Would her attitude change if she found out about his new business venture?

Sometime soon, when he took the next—this time gigantic—corporate step, he'd tell his family, prior to an official announcement. If the current bank negotiations were successful, he'd be purchasing a small suburban shopping centre and have the capital to extend and improve it.

Cassie stood in the shower, combing conditioner through her hair, trying to make sense of the intensity of her responses to Jack. Her normally guarded nature had abandoned her and she had no idea why.

There'd been interest in his captivating eyes despite his reservations about her presence here. For a second or two she wished she'd packed at least one dress and some make-up to wear in the evenings. A mild flirtation with a handsome eligible man to give her self-esteem a boost was tempting.

What was she thinking?

An hour or so ago, she'd been grateful their association would be short-lived. The man scrambled her brain. Clients' family members were taboo. Even those with alluring grass-green eyes, football hero muscles and unmanageable hair.

She was blown away by the table décor when she helped Mel carry the steaming dishes into the dining room. There was even a bottle of wine in an ice bucket near the place settings at one end. This all proved the gulf between her life and theirs. Most evenings at home, she ate from a lap tray while watching television.

Her stomach rumbled as she breathed in the mouth-watering aroma of grilled steak and onion sauce. Until that moment, she hadn't felt hungry at all.

'I'm having rosé to drink,' Mel said as she filled the water glasses. 'How about you? Jack will probably get a beer from the fridge after his run with Sam.'

'A run? In his work boots?'

'He always keeps running shoes in his ute, and it's a regular outing for Sam. He sulks if any of the younger visitors don't have time for at least a short walk.' Mel settled at the head of the table.

'Rosé sounds nice.' Cassie poured the two drinks, sat on her hostess's right and took a slow look around the room. She hadn't seen it, apart from a quick glance in on her arrival.

The antique mantelpiece, the polished sideboard and two of the papered walls held photographs of family. In here they were casual or celebratory. In the family room, school and sporting pictures covered all four walls. Jack was easily recognisable in many of them.

'Does Jack call in often?' She oughtn't to ask, but couldn't hold back.

'It depends on his work. Though he lives twenty minutes from here, most of his regular clients are in the northern and eastern suburbs. *You* understand the drawbacks of driving that distance.'

Cassie sipped her drink and pondered. Travelling time plus fuel-inflated costs influenced choices, especially for pensioners. Word-of-mouth referrals meant the majority of her clients lived north of Adelaide, as she did. Mel's insistence she stayed the Tuesday to Thursday nights in her Woodcroft home meant her quote had been favourable.

'He wasn't too pleased at your sleeping here. He tends to be cautious where I'm concerned. I told him he should be pleased I wasn't alone.'

'It's good he isn't sensitive about showing how much he cares.'

'True, I love that the family are so considerate, just don't like to be reminded I'm getting older. I've warned Jack but he can be tenacious, Cassie. He'll try to sneak subtle questions into general conversation.'

He already had, and wasn't subtle at all.

'He can ask anything he likes.' She didn't have to answer.

Sam's bark echoed from the hall. A moment later he trotted in and curled onto a rug. Jack followed shortly behind, wearing a clean green T-shirt, his boots replaced by black and red runners. Uncapped bottle in hand, he stooped to kiss Mel's forehead.

'Sam was pretty keen today; didn't stop once.'

He sat opposite Cassie, took a deep swig of beer and surveyed her with penetrating interest, causing her to stretch her shoulders. Neither he nor Mel seemed to find it incongruous for him to drink from the bottle at a formally set dinner.

As if reading her thoughts, he carefully poured the remaining liquid into the glass by his cutlery. His sudden grin tripped her heartbeat and sent her pulse racing. She so had to find a way to combat his charm.

'Maybe you should come with us next time. The way your skin glows, I figure you run on a regular basis.'

He thought she glowed? How could one sentence in a casual tone send tiny quivers of pleasure dancing down her spine? Her fingers trembled as she sipped her wine, hoping she didn't choke from the sudden tightness in her throat.

Unless all three housemates were home she ate simple meals and salad. This setting was perfect, the grilled steak delicious and the vegetables slightly crunchy, the way she preferred them. This was how she imagined dining in a fancy restaurant would feel, except Jack would be dressed in appropriate attire.

She tried to picture him in a tailored suit and tie and failed. Yet that niggling thought that he projected only what he wanted people to see persisted. His upbringing almost guaranteed black tie in the wardrobe.

'Cassie, are you with us?' Mel's question startled her.

'Sorry, I was daydreaming, trying to remember when I've had a tastier meal.' She avoided looking across the table, hoping the blush spreading up her neck and cheeks wouldn't be noticeable under the soft lights of the overhead chandelier.

'Thank you. We were discussing my granddaughter Janette in Melbourne, whose baby is due in five weeks. I'm going to be a great-grandmother.'

Cassie was acutely aware of Jack's keen interest, but didn't understand how that concerned her.

'That's so exciting.' An ideal event to strengthen Mel's mental recovery.

'Another sign that life moves on. Deciding to cull my clothes has been freeing for me. I think I'm ready to let go of some items I keep simply because of the past. Would you consider working out a plan to help me downsize in short stages between other commitments?'

Wow, that came out of the blue. She liked Mel and her positive attitude to life, and would happily take on the assignment under normal conditions. Yet Jack's presence added an emotive element; one she'd have to conquer if she accepted.

He'd be occupied elsewhere during the day and hopefully there wouldn't be too many evening visits when she stayed over on weeknights. She'd have to be polite and aloof in his company, professional to a T, and avoid any physical contact.

'I'm sure I can.' As she finished speaking, she turned as if pulled by an invisible thread to Jack's enigmatic green eyes.

Jack hoped his features didn't reveal his conflicting thoughts. Mel living alone in this big house had worried the family since Bob's death. Any attempt to discuss sharing or buying a smaller residence had been firmly rejected so the subject had been dropped. If Cassie's references were as good as Mel claimed, he'd normally have no reservations about her employment.

The problem was him and his instant attraction to her. Hell, he was a mature man and the solution was obvious. Avoid visiting when she was here, and act like the mature man he was supposed to be whenever they met.

'Won't that be inconvenient for you?' He kept his tone as impassive as possible, not easy when her eyes glinted as if she'd read his indecisive mind.

'Many of my clients are retired, often with health problems. Every contract allows for unforeseen contingencies, and I've become extremely adept at rescheduling. There have been times when I've juggled multiple jobs successfully.'

She faced Mel. 'Tomorrow we'll sit down with diaries and discuss what and when.'

'Good, that's settled.' Mel lifted her wineglass in salute and Cassie clinked it with hers as a signal of agreement. Jack followed suit with his near-empty glass of beer, trying to fathom why he felt as if he'd somehow scored a win.

They debated their favourite television shows over a dessert of fresh fruit and whipped cream. Jack teased Mel about her favourite soap operas, claiming she'd converted many of his generation into avid fans. And wondered why Cassie's smile at the interaction wasn't mirrored in her eyes.

He professed not to watch much at all. 'Sport, documentaries or investigative programmes—whatever's on at the time. I'd pick you for a movie girl, Cassie, romance or high adventure.'

'Wrong. Comedies or space sagas, as long as they're well written and acted. If not, I switch channels. I also enjoy home improvement shows.'

'How long do you give them before you click?' He intensified his gaze as he spoke and waited for her answer. Her viewing habits were irrelevant; her character intrigued him.

'That depends on how bad it is, what else is on and how tired I am.'

Clever, evasive answer.

The heat coursing through Cassie's veins had nothing to do with the fake wood fire warming the room, and everything to do with the fact that Jack had turned his attention towards her. His smile and slight raise of one eyebrow hinted he read her true thoughts. He was wrong, couldn't possibly know Mum's favourite programme, always set to tape so never missed, was an enduring Aussie soapy.

Stretching her back, she rose and reached for his bowl. 'I'll stack the dishwasher if you make the hot drinks?'

'None for me,' Mel said. 'I'll watch the news with you then I'm off to bed. I feel tired in the nicest possible way. Tomorrow I might have a baking session.'

Which would leave Cassie alone with Jack unless he called it a night too. She'd had a long day, exacerbated by her body's inexplicable reaction to him, new and unnerving. Could she feign plausible fatigue? How did she somehow know her excuse would be met with scepticism and that eyebrow quirk?

The moment his aunt pushed back her seat to stand, he was there to ease it away and hold her arm. She spoke quietly to him with her back turned to Cassie, and his answering grin stirred a feather-light fluttering in her stomach.

'Always, Mel.' He picked up the empty glasses and large bowl. 'You get settled in the lounge and rest. And I'll expect cherry and ginger cake next visit.'

He headed for the door, his husky chuckle flooding Cassie with a longing for the easy banter that came with deep affection.

'Confident boy, isn't he? Do you think he'd accept something fresh from the bakery?' Mel's tongue-in-cheek remark was accompanied with a gentle laugh.

Cassie took a moment to answer, her mind still processing 'boy'. She doubted there was a single immature cell in Jack Randell's body.

'From what I've seen, he'd settle for home brand plain biscuits to spend time with you, Mel.'

'I admit to resorting to packaged cakes and biscuits since the accident, and he's never even hinted the standard was lower.'

CHAPTER FOUR

JACK WAS FILLING the dishwasher when Cassie brought the remaining china into the kitchen. She kept a good space between them, admiring the way his muscles flexed as he reached up to the bench then bent forward to place each item.

No, you don't. You mustn't.

He pivoted round, as if sensing her appraisal. She wasn't aware of having made a sound, and the gurgle of the coffee machine should have covered any if she had.

'Coffee, tea or hot chocolate?' His sombre eyes and polite tone put her on alert.

'White tea, thank you. I'll finish here.'

Instead of moving away as she expected, he stepped sideways, resting his hands and butt against the bench and crossing one foot over the other. A very masculine stance which should not affect her. Renewed flutters in her stomach proved otherwise.

'I'm not totally convinced about this extra sorting. It might prove too much for her.' Corporate tone. And she knew there was no uncertainty in his mind at all.

'Because you care for her.'

His brow furrowed, his chest expanded and he crossed his arms as if preparing to challenge her reasoning. She forestalled him.

'She's been through a prolonged, trying time. Getting rid of clothes that no longer fit is cathartic and means she's looking forward. I can schedule a few days at a time, and if she finds it tiring or too traumatic we can stop.'

'Your contract will…'

'Have an out clause which allows for either of those as well as unforeseen circumstances.'

Jack wished he could explain why he wanted a longer break before Mel disposed of anything else. His treasured aunt was on a high at the moment, and he feared she might regret the impulse later. Any delaying tactic would be welcome. Unfortunately, his normally active mind was blank.

Well, not really. It was a jumbled mass of thoughts and images of the dark-haired beauty who was regarding him with stunning, empathetic eyes. She had no conception of the perceptive and compassionate woman who'd been the mainstay of the family as long as he could remember. Mel had been the one they'd all turned to for guidance until Bob's death had shaken her belief in life and herself.

'She lost confidence in her own judgement. People she trusted as friends tried to scam her while she was grieving for Bob. Two years ago, an acquaintance claiming to have been a business colleague almost coerced her into signing a contract to put this house on the market.'

He'd been in Queensland that time too. He pushed to his feet, needing action. The exasperated breath he took filled his nostrils with her delicate scent, distracting him. He shook his head, fisted his hands.

'She had the sense to tell my cousin, and he warned the guy off. She wasn't ready then—why now?'

'She may not be.'

What the hell? He glared at her, irked at her composed and conciliatory demeanour.

'Then why the charade?'

Her lips curled and his exasperation dissolved, his taut muscles slumping like Sam after a run. The combination of her beguiling eyes, enticing smile and husky voice was irresistible.

'It's not. She needs to know she's in control after months of relying on you and your family for so much. I'll ensure she doesn't do anything irrational without consultation. *You* have to ensure no one else puts pressure on her in any way.'

Easily done. Whatever was best for his aunt—*his great-aunt*. Accepting she was ageing cut deeper than he'd imagined. The thought that this home might no longer be his family's focal meeting place was mind-numbing. The likelihood had been mentioned occasionally; now it was looming as a reality.

Verbally committed to the new business purchase, he'd be unable to buy the property himself in the foreseeable future. He rubbed the back of his neck in frustration as he turned towards the bench to make the tea and coffee.

On the positive side, staggering the downsizing over months pushed any definite decision into next year. There would be time to find out what Mel really wanted, time for family discussions about the future ownership of the house they all loved. Time to work out an optimum solution for everyone.

For now, strong coffee and reliving today's encounters with Cassie Clarkson would probably keeping him awake tonight, surprisingly not an unpleasant prospect.

He heard the dishwasher start up and glanced sideways to see Cassie pulling on rubber gloves to rinse the wineglasses. Picking up the two drinks, he left her alone, unable to think of a suitable parting remark.

Cassie let the hot water cascade over her hands, allowing treasured memories of her and Mum to flow back. If they were both home, they'd share the cooking and cleaning up, then often settle in front of the television with drinks and home-baked biscuits.

The pain of losing her had barely diminished. The love and laughter they'd shared was as vivid and powerful as ever. She'd been the one who'd taught Cassie to believe in herself and never let anyone demean her, either as a woman or a person.

Jack's bond with his aunt was reminiscent of hers with Mum, as close as that of natural mother and child. She'd give up everything she owned to share life with an ageing Julie Clarkson. Death had denied her the gift she hoped Mel's family appreciated.

She drained the water, flipped the gloves off and squared her shoulders. Jack Randell had been told to play nice and he better had. No more disturbing tingles, and hopefully he'd be busy doing repairs and maintenance a good distance away any time she was here.

Cassie's tea was just right, the after-dinner mints melt-in-the-mouth and Jack's presence in her peripheral vision distracting. Even the TV interview with the hunky action movie star hadn't grabbed her attention. Yesterday it might have. She shifted position, curling her legs up, angling her body away from the big armchair.

A distinct *humph* made her swing round and catch him frowning at the weather pattern on the screen. The presenter was forecasting steady rain for two days.

'That cans tomorrow's lawn mowing. Looks like I'll be working through that list of yours, Mel. And any other chores you think of.'

'Are you sure, Jack? There must be…'

'The inside jobs booked for next week can't be brought forward. I'm all yours.'

Those three little words created unfamiliar and unwarranted sensations in Cassie's abdomen. Like a ferry ride in rough weather, exhilarating and heart-stopping. They spread warmth to her toes and up to her cheeks, and she quickly looked away. Bending her head, she sipped her drink, hoping he'd think any colour came from its heat.

Mel muted the sound and left the remote on the coffee table.

'Do you want to stay tonight, Jack?'

Her innocent question almost had Cassie choking as she swallowed. Jack sleeping in the room across the hall from hers. Jack showering in the bathroom one wall away. Jack...

What was the matter with her?

She shared a house with two men, and didn't turn a hair if they wandered around draped in a towel.

'I'll go home, thanks. How about I pick up breakfast in the morning? Special treat.'

'Ooh, yes, delicious egg and bacon rolls, full of calories and cholesterol. Delightfully wicked at my age,' Mel enthused. 'Just don't tell my doctor.'

'It's a deal.'

'With that pleasant thought to send me to sleep, I'll say goodnight. Thank you both for a lovely day, the best I've had for ages.' After turning the sound up again, she left the room.

Persuasive advertisements urged them to buy, buy, buy, backed up by jarring music. Cassie finished her drink, held on to her mug and tried to formulate an intelligent topic opener. Nothing came to mind.

'Yawning might help.'

Startled, she almost dropped her mug. His smooth-as-silk deep timbre coiled around her heart, enthralling her. His wide smile and the provocative gleam in his eyes activated warning signals in her brain.

She set her mug down, clenched her stomach and mentally strengthened her resolve. If he thought she'd be easy to charm, he was in for a disappointment. The foolish romantic side of her hoped he'd try.

'Help what?'

His grin widened. 'Convince me you're tired and want to go to bed.'

Her sucked-in gasp wasn't nearly as incriminating as the heatwave that swept over her skin. The surge of desire at his unintended suggestion stunned her, left her speechless and fighting for breath.

He caught the double meaning, chuckled, and that darn Outback scene flashed into her head. She blinked it away. Too late—he'd noticed.

In a rapid switch, he leant forward, hands clasped between his knees. His now sombre expression matched the thoughtful contemplation in his eyes. She drew in a steadying lungful of air and waited.

'Your choice, Cassie. I can leave now or we can a while. We're going to see quite a lot of each other in the next few months. The more at ease we are together, the happier Mel will be.'

Easy for you to say, Jack Randell. Your hormones aren't going crazy whenever you're near me.

She wriggled back into the corner.

As if that little bit of distance will diminish his potency.

Her brain scrabbled for an intelligent question.

'How long have your parents lived in Queensland?' Background stuff, not *too* personal. If he followed suit, her disclosures could be of similar ilk.

All Jack had gained was a few minutes' grace so why the crazy, unwarranted *zing* of success? He felt muscles he hadn't noticed become taut, loosen, and wished he were on the settee beside her. Close enough to inhale her alluring aroma. Not tonight, perhaps—*would there ever be a good time?* And what had happened to his *stay away when she's here* decision?

'Nine years. My mother hated Adelaide winters, always spent part of them up north with *her* family. She met Dad on a spring cruise to the Pacific Islands and married him six months later.'

He relaxed into his chair, legs outstretched, arms loose on the side arms. When Sam walked over and plopped beside him, head over Jack's ankles, he bent to scratch the dog's ears.

'She put up with the cold because she loved him and he was an integral part of the family law firm, handling the accounting department. Once my brother, sister and I were self-sufficient, Dad resigned, sold up and they relocated to Queensland. He works for himself with an assistant. Less pressure, more time together.'

An abridged version, omitting his mother's depression in his teens, and his struggle to avoid becoming ensnared in the Randell legal world.

'Mel said most of the family find a reason to visit them during the year.'

Jack's gut tightened at the faint tremor in Cassie's voice and the wistful expression in her eyes. Quickly blinked away.

'Especially during our winter. Your family aren't within easy contact?'

She stilled, broke eye contact and her shoulders pressed back. Away from him or the question?

'No.' Steady. Resolute. 'Mum died four years ago. There are no other relatives.'

Her stark sentences left him dumbfounded, mouth open, back stiffening as he jerked forward.

'No one?'

No way could he envisage a world without his parents, aunts and uncles, his siblings and numerous cousins. Noisy, sometimes boisterous get-togethers had always been an integral part of his life.

He'd rebelled at the pressure from his father and mother to conform, to gain entry to law school and follow the path they'd chosen for him. There'd been loud, occasionally acrimonious arguments about his partying and seeming lack of study even though his grades were always high. Even at those times, there'd always been someone there for him, often a choice of many. They might not have agreed with his decisions but they'd given him moral support.

Watching the obvious change in his expression, he saw chagrin flood her face as she gave a choking laugh.

'That came out as if I'm alone and abandoned. I never felt deprived because there was only the two of us, and I have a very supportive group of friends.'

'You live alone?' Spoken instinctively. He hadn't meant to ask; it went beyond the bounds he'd set himself.

'I share a house with two school friends. And you?'

'Just me in my place near the beach at Port Noarlunga South.'

'Do you surf?'

'Best way to get the adrenaline going in the morning, though work takes precedence these days.' Actually, it was the second best, and the sudden thought of sharing the first with her sent his pulse racing.

'I tried years ago. Couldn't see the attraction of getting dumped every time I tried to stand up.'

The sudden sparkle in her eyes belied her words; she'd enjoyed the experience. He imagined her in a sleek wetsuit and his body responded, causing him to shift in his chair.

'Maybe you need an expert to teach you.' Had he meant that to sound like an offer? Yes, if she was still around when the weather warmed up.

'Or better balance.'

A strident voice in increased decibels made both heads swing towards the television.

'That certainly won't entice me into their store.' Jack reached for the remote, pressed off, and said with reluctance, 'Time I went home.'

He ensured Sam was settled on his bed in the family room while Cassie took the mugs to the kitchen. She seemed reluctant to approach him as he waited, hand on the back doorknob, to say goodbye. Was she regretting the disclosure of personal aspects of her life?

'Lock up behind me, Cassie. I'll see you in the morning.'

'Goodnight, Jack.'

He closed the door, waited in the cold air until he heard the key turn, then walked to his ute.

Cassie blew out a huff of air, ashamed for the awkwardness that had stopped her from going too near as he'd left. Little as it was, she'd revealed more to him than she ever had to anyone she didn't know well.

She waited until he'd driven off then went to her room, turning off lights on the way. After mulling over their conversation, she drifted in and out of restless sleep, trying to make sense of her uncontrollable responses.

Early next morning Jack parked at the side of the house and sat contemplating the vegetable patch where he and his contemporaries had spent so many happy hours. Whatever happened, he'd always have those cherished memories.

Hearing Sam's bark alongside, he hopped out and ruffled the dog's fur. He was rewarded with a frantic wagging of the tail and avid attempts to jump up and lick any flesh Sam's wet tongue could reach.

'Easy, boy. I've already had my shower.'

Sam dropped and raced to the rear of the vehicle. Following, Jack found Cassie, fingers clenched, staring wide-eyed at his ute as if she'd never seen one before.

He walked to her side, checking her line of vision. Couldn't see anything wrong.

'Good morning, Cassie. Am I missing something?'

'Mel said you had a ute.' It sounded like an accusation. 'That's…'

'A silver twin cab, multipurpose utility with accessories. I got a great deal in an end-of-year sale last June. Good for work, family and camping.'

'It's so big. And clean.'

His instant roar of laughter made her blink and her eyes became dreamy, as if recalling a treasured scene.

'I'll take that in the spirit I believe you meant. It handles the biggest and heaviest loads I carry, fits five people and goes off-road like a dune buggy.' He put his hand on the polished tailgate and captured her gaze with his. 'And I take good care of what's mine.'

She didn't stir, didn't react. Thankfully, she didn't break eye contact, allowing him to see the flickering of awareness, along with the soft blush on her cheeks. He'd noticed the faint colouring last night, but failed to detect the reason. Undeserved macho pride flared, triggering an impulse to puff out his chest, a desire to caress her silken skin.

Sam's nudge to his leg broke the spell. *For now.* Sooner rather than later they'd touch again. He wouldn't deliberately engineer it but if a chance arose he'd take it without hesitation.

'Better get inside while the rolls are still hot.'

'Mel was setting out the coffee mugs when I left. She's looking forward to your arrival.'

'And you?'

He'd bring breakfast every day to earn a sweet smile like the one she gave him now.

'What do you think? Walking Sam's given me an appetite, so I hope you brought enough.' She shivered as a few raindrops fell on her head. 'Come on, Sam.'

She moved towards the house. The dog hesitated, looked up at him then took off.

He grabbed the bags from the front seat, and caught up in time to open the door for Cassie. A hint of peaches hung in the air as she passed him, sweet as the ones from the tree at the bottom of the garden. Mentally telling himself to get a grip, he followed her, nearly tripping on the eager dog who'd stopped to shake off the rain.

CHAPTER FIVE

CASSIE WASHED HER hands before following Jack into the lounge, where Mel was waiting with a pot of freshly brewed coffee. She heard him tease her for insisting they ate from the wrappers.

'Fast food always tastes better this way. I have great memories of sitting on the beach, eating fish and chips from butcher's paper and fighting off the seagulls.'

'It was always fun, wasn't it? We'll do it again when the weather clears. Today it's indoor chores.'

The tenderness in his voice, and the way his features softened with affection as he spoke to his great-aunt, caused a lump in her throat. Moments like the ones they referred to were a major part of her treasured memories.

She stared through the window, remembering the unconditional love she and Mum had shared, so much joy and few regrets. The past couldn't be changed. Today was the time that mattered, and she had a task for Jack if he was willing.

'I noticed some of the light fittings are dusty, Jack. Do you have the time to clean them?'

'Checking lights comes under downsizing?' A sceptical look accompanied his gentle dig.

'Under due diligence and caring, a courtesy for clients. In your line of work, you should know most people don't notice the grime until they have to replace the bulbs or tubes.'

'True. Consider all the house fittings on my list.'

The three of them chatted about the house and garden as they ate, and Cassie learned how Bob had relished teaching the younger generation the tool and gardening crafts that Jack had turned into a profession. That his father had wanted him to study law and become his uncle's partner didn't surprise her; his telling her did.

Mel's mobile rang, and she answered. 'Well, you know I'd love to normally but at the moment…'

Cassie tapped her arm.

'Hang on, Dot.' Mel held the phone to her chest. 'The Mortons have invited me to go with them and visit a friend in Murray Bridge for her birthday.'

'Say yes.'

'I can't. It's overnight and you're here. We've got…'

'Other days for sorting. Say yes.'

She was aware of Jack's shoulders straightening and his head snapping back, let it slide. No chance for even a moment of happiness should ever be missed. Mum was proof the future was unpredictable.

'Are you sure?' Mel glanced from her to Jack, who nodded. For Cassie, her grateful smile was worth rearranging her schedule.

After accepting the invitation, Mel switched off her phone and sank back in her seat looking a little dazed.

'They'll be here at nine-thirty.'

Jack lifted the coffeepot to refill her cup. 'Packing for one night won't take long, so you've got plenty of time to finish your meal.'

She stopped his action and laughed. 'Not advisable before a long car trip.'

'Cassie?' He held up the pot and smiled, making her pulse blip. As soon as she'd finished labelling the outfits Mel had selected, and listed everything, she'd leave. On Friday there'd be her and her employer and no heart-melting distraction.

The Mortons were punctual, and the rain had eased to a drizzle as they settled Mel into the back seat of the car and waved goodbye. Cassie shook off the drops from her hair before re-entering the house, trying not to dwell on being alone with Jack. This morning his cologne was fresher, more enticing, and hard to ignore from right behind her.

'Thank you, Cassie. She'll have a great time, hasn't been out much, apart from with family, for a while.'

His voice was deeper, as if emotional. Giving her hair a final flick with her fingers, she let her hands fall to her sides as she looked up into speculative green eyes. Did he still harbour suspicion of her after their talk last night? Better for them both if he did and kept distance between them.

'It's no big deal. Would you like me to prepare something for lunch later?'

'That'll be great. I'll get my tools and start upstairs; you can select the music.' He paused as if to add something, dropped his gaze to her lips for a moment then walked out.

There were few modern CDs in Mel's collection of film soundtracks, classical and compilations. She chose one with familiar songs, a favourite old movie of Mum's.

Although she couldn't see Jack, soft sounds filtered down from the second floor, disturbing her concentration. She chastised her heart for beating faster at the thought of him standing on his steps in the bathroom to clean the fluorescent lights. She knew how easily the tubes shattered and how sharp the shards could be. There was no logical reason to worry. He was a competent tradesman and could take care of himself.

Taking extra care had nothing to do with Jack's competency. He was alone in the house with the most distracting woman he had ever met. She'd kept him awake last night and invaded his dreams when he'd finally fallen asleep.

Cassie was a mystery the pragmatic part of his temperament was determined to solve. How, he hadn't figured out yet. Getting too close might be painful for them both. On the surface, she was bright and open, but behind her incredible dark brown eyes lay painful secrets.

As long as they didn't affect her employment with Mel he shouldn't give a damn. Yet he did. He wanted to know why sorrow veiled them from view, why she turned away when he and his aunt shared fun moments. To know why an attractive, intelligent twenty-seven-year-old woman had chosen a profession that basically limited her clientele to the older generation.

He focused on reattaching the light fitting in the back bedroom, checked all bulbs lit up, and grinned as a song he hadn't heard for a long time drifted up the stairway. He made a mental note to show Cassie where the switches were for the speakers he'd installed on the second floor so she could listen while working up there.

She obviously shared the same taste in music as Mel and Bob. This house had rarely been silent and he'd subliminally learnt the lyrics of so many musicals, sometimes causing him embarrassment in front of his teenage friends.

Now he was secure in who and what he was, and didn't care who heard him. Mel was well on the way to being fully fit and socially active. The investment he was negotiating was on track. On the negative side were the possible sale of the house and his Cassie-activated libido. Somehow, he'd come to terms with both problems.

He picked up his folded steps and toolkit and headed for the next room, singing along with the rousing action hero.

Something was different. It took Cassie a minute or so to realise it was Jack, singing along with the CD in an assured pleasant tone as he moved from room to room upstairs. She couldn't prevent her imagination picturing him taking the lead, and gliding across the screen with the beautiful heroine.

She moved along the clothes racks, lightly brushing the

garments, loving the different fabrics, the smooth silks and satins, the elaborate brocades and the delicate lace designs. None showed signs of wear, all hung beautifully as if new; such a difference to some of her chain store brand purchases. It was time she added a few quality items that would never date her wardrobe.

She appreciated these were not just clothes. This was a timeline spanning many years of happy marriage. When originally bought, each outfit represented a birthday, an engagement or wedding, a business celebration. Every piece held memories; now they'd create new ones for delighted buyers who'd dreamt of owning designer quality.

The romantic love songs playing in the background suited her mood. In her mind, she could see the colourful costumes twirling from enthusiastic dancing, and Jack swinging the heroine off her feet and spinning her round.

Believing he wouldn't hear, she felt confident enough to sing softly, letting herself be drawn into the magic. Keeping time, she almost skipped into the kitchen for a glass of water prior to settling to input her handwritten notes into the computer.

She drank slowly, watching the rain fall on the well-tended garden. This was a peaceful home, a haven of love and sharing. The current song ended in a crescendo then silence, and she recalled the hero dipping his head to kiss the heroine in that quiet moment.

Without warning, the hairs on her nape stood up, tingles skittled down her spine. She pivoted to confront Jack in the doorway with a wide grin on his handsome face. He'd heard her singing. Warmth flooded her cheeks, and the urge to run was stymied by an overwhelming desire to see what he'd do next.

Pinning her with riveting green eyes, he walked forward as the introduction to the next song started. Cassie froze. This was a hero's serenade. A half step back and she was pinned between his mesmerising gaze and the sink behind her.

Captivated, she allowed him to take her hand and draw her closer, caught her breath as he placed his free hand on her waist and led her into a dance. He guided her with gentle expertise, and she followed as if they'd been partners for ever. His eyes gleamed like the rain-kissed leaves outside, and his work-rough palm gently grazed hers, evoking tiny quivers that radiated and grew.

Like a prince and princess in a fairy tale they glided around the floor, her heart beating time with the music. The heady mixture of male and sandalwood heightened her senses. The soft pressure of his thigh against hers as they spun and twirled stirred new and thrilling sensations.

Even beautiful dreams had to end and theirs came too soon. They stilled, eyes locked and bodies swaying to unheard music. His lips parted, his head bent towards hers.

A new song, rough and loud, by the whole male cast, ruptured the silence and severed the spell that bound them.

Jack moved away from Cassie, his hands reluctant to break the connection, his body craving closer contact. Her quiet singing had drawn him from the second floor, with no concept of his intent.

He'd known the second she'd become aware of him, and couldn't stop the smile from forming as she'd turned. Her beautiful, sparkling brown eyes had widened with uncertainty, a sweet blush coloured her cheeks and her mouth formed an O as she sucked in an unsteady breath.

His heart had hammered on the short journey across the room and his stomach tightened in anticipation of an energy zap like last time they'd touched. Today he fully intended to hold on, discover where it led.

The opening chords had sounded as he'd reached for her hand, and he'd relished the *zing* that sizzled along his veins.

With his free hand on her waist, he'd begun to waltz her around the kitchen, keeping steady eye contact. Mentally he'd harmonised with the love-struck singer.

His heartbeat had surged as Cassie synchronised with his steps. They and his guidance were automatic; his mind and body were totally focused on the woman in his arms. Soft and pliant, she'd moulded to his form, her peach scent beguiling.

The music ended, and he couldn't let go. Her eyes had invited and he'd accepted, bending his head towards her.

A loud, raucous drum roll filled the air, followed by grating unintelligible words. Cassie blinked as if startled, and arched away. He shuffled back, delayed letting go as long as possible. Once he did, this magical moment would be over.

She seemed as dazed as he felt, her arms limp at her sides and her chest rising and falling in agitation. She swallowed, had difficulty speaking.

'It's... I... You want coffee?'

Way down on his list. Why the hell couldn't he form coherent words? He'd had no trouble singing someone else's.

'Give me five minutes. See you in the lounge.' He walked out, trying to remember where he'd been heading, and why, when he'd heard her singing.

The seven minutes he took allowed Cassie to regain composure and perspective, at least on the outside where it showed. She'd been caught up in a fantasy, beguiled by his charisma, lost in the moment. In future, she'd be prepared and resist him with dignity and grace.

Who are you kidding? Your resolve will crumble at his slightest touch.

So she'd avoid contact while she finished the tasks agreed with Mel earlier. Hopefully he'd have prearranged activities elsewhere on Friday, and that would be her last day until the next session here.

Mum had always stressed the importance of decorum. An achievable state until he walked in with sombre eyes and a rueful smile, and her pulse dumped composure for roller coaster speed. He picked up his steaming mug and settled into the armchair as if it were made for him. Sam curled at his feet, making a perfect picture of master and faithful hound.

English was a vast language so why was her mind blank of a conversation opener?

What would you like for lunch? Thank you for the dance. It was heaven in your arms.

'I'm sorry.'

His words hit like a soccer punch to her stomach and she recoiled, pressing into the cushions. She squeezed her eyes shut and dug her nails into her palms. He regretted the moment she'd always treasure.

'No.' *Clunk.* The two sounds were simultaneous.

Her eyes flew open. Jack thrust forward, hands spread in appeal. His mug was on the table surrounded by splashes of coffee.

'Not for the memorable dance. I'm sorry if I've made you feel uncomfortable, Cassie. That was never the intention, though I have to admit I'm not sure what was.'

Her pain dissolved in the warm glow that soothed as it radiated from her abdomen. He'd enjoyed what they'd shared. It had been one of life's inexplicable happenings which must never recur.

She tried to justify her own response. 'Getting caught up in the music. Having all that open space. But you're related to my employer so I should have refused.'

His fingers gripped the chair arms, his lips thinned and his eyes narrowed. 'Are *you* sorry, Cassie?'

'No, it was...' How could she describe her feelings without revealing her vulnerability?

She sprang to her feet. 'As you said, memorable. A spur

of the moment, one-off event. I'll get a cloth to wipe the table.'

It was as if her muscles gave a sigh of relief as she quickened her pace to the kitchen. On the slower return trip, she ran task-related topics through her head.

Jack's mind ran a similar course in a methodical manner, at odds with his erratic emotions. He adored Mel, and would never do anything that might embarrass or hurt her. Coming on to the woman she'd hired to help her move on in her life definitely came under that banner.

Cassie's words indicated a strict code of work ethics, so she'd be as spooked by the attraction that flared between them as he was, and seemed as powerless as he to resist.

His desire to learn more about her was undeniable. His gut feeling said whatever she hid didn't necessarily relate to her profession. That was really none of his business; he had secrets of his own he'd never shared with anyone.

It didn't stop him avidly waiting for her to reappear, for his muscles tensing and his heart skipping beats when she did. Remorse shamed him as she knelt by the table to mop up. She'd raced from the room before he had the chance to say he'd go.

'My mess; I should be cleaning it. Thank you, Cassie.'

'You're welcome. Do you want a refill?' She smiled, and his breath caught in his throat. He'd almost kissed those delectable lips today, couldn't guarantee not to if the chance arose again.

'No, this will do.' He drank almost half in one swallow. 'What's your next task?'

'Bring down Mel's footwear, list, label and double-check everything. Then I'll go home.'

Rapid control prevented another coffee spill, this time on himself. 'Why?'

'Because it'll be easier if everything's in one room. There's stickers and she can—'

'I get that. Why are you going home?'

'I'll have done all I can without her being here. She can make decisions at leisure tomorrow, and when I come back on Friday I'll finalise her lists and print out copies.'

His breath caught in his throat, trapped by the lump that clogged his air passage. There'd be no telling when he'd see her again. For someone who'd rarely had a problem swaying opponents to his point of view, he was confounded by his inability to reply.

A fruitless search for her on social media before retiring last night had irked but not discouraged him. Offering to recommend her services would provide him with her number, and save him having to explain why if he asked Mel.

'So I'd better get started. Does lunch at one suit you?'

Lunch? It didn't help that she was so eager to leave. How had life become so complicated in less than twenty-four hours?

'Yeah, one's fine.' He watched her walk out, glared at his coffee mug as if it were responsible then drained it. Couldn't figure why he was annoyed at himself.

He stooped to ruffle Sam's fur. 'Come on, Sam.' Pushing himself to his feet, he headed back upstairs, the dog close behind him.

CHAPTER SIX

CLEANING LIGHT FITTINGS and replacing globes was routine for Jack, needing care without much concentration. If he encouraged Cassie to talk about her work over lunch, she might inadvertently divulge more about herself. Personal questions needed a different atmosphere. The spark of an idea grew into a full plan.

He'd never felt such a spontaneous desire for a woman before. The doubts he still harboured stemmed from previous attempts to con Mel and, if he were honest, his own experiences with women seeking a rich husband.

When she walked in, he instinctively smiled, his chest tightened and his pulse raced. It was as if she brought sunshine, even though it was raining outside.

'Ham sandwiches ready when you are.' Brown eyes shining, she gazed around the sunroom. 'Every home should have a room like this, bright and sunny most mornings and snug and intimate in the evenings.'

To Jack it had always been the small room at the front of the house, containing a sewing machine, long table, odd chairs and a large lockable cupboard where Christmas and birthday presents were hidden. A woman's room as opposed to Bob's workshop, where he'd spent so many happy, productive hours learning handyman skills.

'Good timing. Can you pass me that bulb from the table, and stay to switch on when I say?'

He grinned when it lit up, and stepped down. 'Never can tell with these old fittings. What are you thinking?'

Her head was at a slight tilt as she studied the now sparkling chandelier, her expression reflective. He followed her gaze.

'How hard it must be to face the prospect of leaving a house you decorated, where many of the fittings and furniture were chosen as a couple. All of them would have been selected with the aim of providing a loving family home.'

Her voice grew softer and emotional towards the end, as if she were describing a personal memory. Their eyes met and he glimpsed a fleeting sadness that proved him right.

'She and Bob moved in two years after their wedding, and renovated every room together. She never wanted to live anywhere else and always said she'd be here till…'

He faltered. When Mel made the statement it sounded right. He couldn't bring himself to say the final words.

'I've been helping with repairs for years and never considered any of their belongings in quite that way before. It makes a difference. Thank you, Cassie.'

A new concept flared like a beacon, breaking through the gloom of Mel's health-related intention to move. Too new and undefined to share. They could install brighter lights, rails, new, easier to manage taps and other safety measures. Redesign the downstairs bathroom if need be. Mel was sure to agree. The changes would enable her to stay as long as she really wanted. For many, many years if he had his way.

If that was what she really wanted—that was the pivotal point. And there was no denying she did need someone living with her. He'd make notes and talk to her tomorrow.

'Let's have lunch.'

He ushered Cassie from the room, eager for food and talk. Sinking into his usual spot, plate of sandwiches on his lap and cold beer within reach, he relished the comfort he felt from being in Bob's favourite chair. If Mel ever decided to let it go, he'd take it home, make it his. For now, he'd settle for the contentment it evoked right here.

He liked that Cassie had chosen a favourite spot too. She looked good, snug against the corner of the settee, outwardly at ease though her breathing was slow and controlled and the fingers on her right hand were curled but not clenched.

Lifting his drink, he took a long swallow and dived in.

'Where do you live? Mel mentioned north of the city.' He watched for signs of hesitation or evasion. There were none.

'Oakden—twenty minutes from the city in good traffic.'

'So why take a job involving possibly two hours' driving daily?'

'I wouldn't normally.' She matched his gaze, letting him know she wasn't fooled by his seemingly casual questions.

'Mel called me and we met for coffee in the city. I advised her to find someone local to make it affordable and she offered accommodation Tuesday to Thursday.'

'You accepted the job without coming here?'

Her laugh was unexpected and accompanied by a tantalising sparkle in her eyes. The inevitable ripple through him was accompanied by a stomach clench and an instant acceleration of his pulse.

'Would you estimate on a job unseen? I came for lunch, toured the house at her insistence and visited a couple of wineries on the way. My quote included an allowance for food and board.'

Jack bit into his sandwich and chewed slowly as he considered her answers, which were open and plausible. The same could apply to the woman who'd conned his mother into investing in a dodgy jewellery business. And the man who'd plagued Mel for weeks after Bob's death about a special memorial site until she'd told Jack and he'd informed the police.

'Have dinner with me tonight.' He realised he'd voiced his thoughts when he heard the words and saw her startled reaction.

'What?' She'd jerked forward, her sandwich held in the

air, her brown eyes darkening, widening with astonishment. Big and beautiful, drawing him in.

'You were supposed to stay here, so you can't have anything planned.'

'Why? You don't trust me.' Defensive. Wary.

'I never said that. Let me get to know you. And you, me. I'll pick you up at seven and we'll go somewhere local.'

Cassie stared at the nonchalant figure watching her with a resolute expression. This didn't have the feel of an *I-like-you* invitation, more a *come-into-my-web* trap.

She'd be crazy to accept. Probably regret saying yes, definitely would if she declined. If she agreed, and gave him limited information, maybe he'd be satisfied and let her do her job unhindered.

That's it, Cassie. Logical, reasonable thoughts to help you make a rational decision.

'Strictly platonic.'

And that tells him you've been thinking the opposite.

Her mind registered the sudden tension in his shoulders and neck, her eyes only saw the quick flare in his green eyes that sparked a heated response in her abdomen.

'Absolutely. I'll need your address and phone number.' He reached for his mobile on the shelf beside him.

She hesitated. 'It's a long way to come. Couldn't we meet somewhere between?'

'No way. I invite a girl to dinner, I pick her up and ensure she gets home safely.' He scrolled to his contacts list, thumbed in her name and silently waited for her reply.

After entering the information, he thanked her then added, 'You'll need my number. In case.'

There was a hint of caution in his voice, as if to say it should not be used for a change of mind. Once she'd closed her phone, he relaxed. Not in an arrogant way, more like quiet satisfaction.

That was exactly how Jack felt, as if he'd negotiated a truce. Keeping it was up to him.

Thirty-six minutes past two. Cassie shut everything down, leant her elbows on the table and pressed her face between joined thumbs and fingers. Closing her eyes didn't make her problem vanish. Instead, it conjured up images of Jack, and the widely diverse expressions in his compelling green eyes. How many women had found themselves succumbing to their spell?

She straightened her back, shook her head and exhaled loudly. Taking the new lists from the printer, she turned to look at the neat rows of footwear. Cassie's collection fitted in the bottom of her wardrobe; Mel's began next to the first leg of the billiard table and ended over halfway along the opposite wall. A reminder of the social chasm between this family and her, no matter how friendly they were.

Why was she sitting here daydreaming instead of packing up and heading home? Because, even allowing for traffic, showering or a leisurely bubble bath and getting ready for—not a date—there'd still be time to kill.

Had she made the right decision? Conversation wouldn't allay Jack's fears about the effect more sorting and decision-making might have on his great-aunt. Physically seeing her happy at being organised and prepared for the future would. So why had she succumbed to his invitation? Because she'd been spellbound by his tingling touch, his deep alluring voice that hijacked her pulse and his mesmerising green eyes.

Arching her spine, she brushed away those disconcerting images. Perhaps taking a detour to her local shopping centre to browse for a while would settle her. Better than being dressed to go early and pacing the floor. Drat the man and his innate appeal.

* * *

He was in the downstairs bathroom, taking measurements and writing them in a thick red diary, when she went to say goodbye. As far as she could tell, there was nothing in the room that needed adjusting or repairing.

Jack didn't enlighten her, merely placed the book on the washstand and leant against it, arms folded, body at ease.

'All done?'

'Until Friday. I've left printed sheets and highlighters by her computer.'

And I'm not sure about tonight.

Thankfully, he didn't pick up on her reservations. 'I heard you make quite a few trips up and down. How many pairs are there?'

'More than I'll ever wear out. High quality and in good condition.'

His crackly laugh shimmied up and down her spine. An Outback trip to authenticate her fantasy was now on her bucket list, earmarked for this summer.

'What is it with women and shoes? You seem to need a pair for every outfit.'

'Hey, no stereotyping. It's a personal trait. And what about men and their gadgets?'

His hands came up in surrender. Without warning, she imagined them caressing her into submission, and felt her skin burn at the thought. His smile and sparkling eyes did nothing to ease the heat or embarrassment, especially when buffalo grass-green darkened to near black.

'I'd better go. I'll see you tonight.' She swung away, eager to put distance between them.

'Seven o'clock, Cassie. I'm looking forward to the evening.'

Less than a minute later Jack heard the back door close. That was the quickest exit he'd seen anywhere for a while. And what the hell had caused that beautiful deep red blush?

He recalled their discussion without finding a reason.

There'd been gentle teasing, nothing awkward. He let it go, not wanting to upset her for Mel's sake. His aunt's happiness was paramount, not that it meant he wouldn't try to find out more about Cassie Clarkson.

Opening his diary and picking up his tape measure, he tried to concentrate on his renovation plan. His head refused to cooperate, persistently flicking up images of Cassie. After he'd wrongly read a figure twice, he took Sam for a run, followed by a strong black coffee.

Cassie was ready at quarter to seven. She turned the television on then off, not wanting it to drown out his arrival. Believing he'd come early so she'd invite him in, *her* plan was to meet him outside.

Repeated brushing of her hair hadn't changed its style, and peeking through the blinds didn't make him miraculously appear.

Checking the hall clock against her wristwatch proved both were aligned. Going to the kitchen for a glass of water to ease her dry throat took one minute. Checking her reflection in the mirror above the lounge mantelpiece simply gave her cause to chastise herself for being so uptight.

Although there was no denying the chemistry between them, she sensed his resolve to avoid any form of close relationship. This wasn't a date; he'd stated the objective was to become more at ease with each other for his aunt's sake. And she could hardly complain when having a shining knight's protection was most women's fantasy come true. It was even on her own *some-day-in-the future* list.

Was Jack prepared to talk about his relatives, as in one-for-one questions? The snippets she'd learned from Mel had stirred her interest in the close-knit, yet diverse family.

She slipped on her jacket and went to the window overlooking the street. Three minutes later—it seemed so much longer—the ute drove past, slowing down to park by the kerb. Feeling an almost childish eagerness, she picked up her handbag, walked out and was halfway down the driveway when he strode into view.

If this *wasn't* a date, heaven help the women he dressed to impress. The combination of royal blue shirt, navy tie, dark denim jeans and brown suede jacket could feature in any classy magazine. His shiny black boots looked new, and his hair... She didn't think there was a woman alive who wouldn't be tempted to finger comb his unruly brown hair into place. Again and again.

His sensual wide mouth curved into a stunning smile that triggered warning flashes in her brain.

'Hi, Cassie, I'm glad to see you too.'

Had she smiled first? It was an automatic female response to an attractive male coming to greet her.

Taking her arm, he led her to the vehicle, clicking the locks on the way. Leaning past to open the door, he stayed close enough to assist her if needed. His sandalwood cologne teased her nostrils, inviting her to sway towards him and inhale deeper.

She resisted, tossed her bag onto the seat and reached for the handle high on the inside of the cab. With the other hand on the back of the seat, she stepped up and swung in, his light guiding touch arousing quivers she had no way of hiding.

Her 'Thank you' sounded breathy and choked. His 'You're welcome' resonated with an undertone she couldn't identify.

Jack walked around the bonnet, chest tight and pulse racing. He'd thought parking in the next street until seven minutes before his due arrival was a good idea. Manners would dictate he be invited in while she put on her coat, and introduce him to her housemates if they were there.

Instead he'd been thwarted in the driveway by a captivating beauty in a fitted red woollen dress that covered her knees, black tights and heeled red ankle boots. Her unbuttoned thick navy jacket fell to her hips.

He'd fought for air as his gaze met enticing brown eyes, enhanced with make-up for the first time since they'd met. She'd also added an unneeded—as far as he was concerned—slight touch of gloss to her red lips. Her sudden smile had sent a surge of heat zapping from head to foot, and all points east to west.

Standing behind her as she boosted herself into his ute had allowed him a closer view of her curvaceous hips and shapely legs, with predictable results. So much for keeping calm and in control. He'd become aware of his gritted teeth and set jaw, and with effort managed a stilted reply to her thanks. Necessity ensured he take a moment to refill his lungs before opening his door and climbing in beside her.

He flicked her a glance, checked his mirror and pulled away. 'You look nice, Cassie.'

Idiot. That was an understatement and a half. She was delightful, exquisite. The line between knowledge for Mel's protection and discovering the woman behind the professional persona became more blurred with every breath, every look. Every touch.

'Thank you. Where are we going?'

Her voice captivated him, pleasurable to hear with its unique edge. And he had all evening to enjoy the sweet sound.

'North Adelaide. Australian menu. Do you have any preferences or absolute dislikes?'

'Apart from very hot or spicy, I'll eat almost anything. Mum and I enjoyed finding new venues and sampling different foods.'

He caught the tense. Before her mother died, leaving her alone. That might be a subject best left for another occasion.

Traffic was light and they drove in comfortable silence towards the city. She hadn't mentioned her father so he wouldn't. He'd blow any chance of her opening up to him if the man had treated them badly.

Cassie had been to many of the diverse cultural restaurants in O'Connell Street and the surrounding area. She regretted not having been for a while. Her memories from here were all happy, comforting her when she became nostalgic.

She caught her breath when Jack slowed and activated his left indicator as they approached a two-storey colonial-style building. The wide steps with their Roman-style columns, peaked eaves and romantic balconies were reminiscent of a classic Hollywood movie. Was that their destination or was he looking for somewhere to park?

Jack made another left turn into the low brick-walled enclosure. It *was* here. A magnificent hotel she'd always admired yet thought too grand for the casual nights out she'd shared with Mum and friends.

There were plenty of spaces yet Jack drove to the one by the far wall and deftly reversed in. His consideration earned him Brownie points as she remembered numerous frustrating times trying to see beyond a vehicle this size at shopping centres.

'Hang on.' His soft tone negated the order in his words.

She unfastened her seatbelt and waited for him to open her door. The touch of his warm fingers clasping hers sent a tremble way down past her knees. She held tight as she alighted, praying they wouldn't buckle and send her sprawling or into his arms. Which wouldn't be a bad thing. Would it?

As if he sensed her apprehension, he placed his free arm around her, holding her steady as he closed the door and activated the lock. She didn't demur when he kept it there to guide her to the entrance and up the steps.

CHAPTER SEVEN

IT WAS COSY and warm inside, and they were ushered to a table next to a decorative brick wall and under a glass awning. Cassie loved the padded plush black seats, and the way the softened lighting gave the whole room a subdued ambience. It was ideal for private conversations.

Both declined pre-dinner drinks and enjoyed a lively discussion of the menu, eventually agreeing on entrée and main course. Dessert would depend on the size of the first two courses.

'You'd easily manage all three, wouldn't you?' Cassie bantered after they'd given their order. 'Your job must build up an appetite.'

'Most days the work's steady rather than strenuous. I try not to overindulge, with an exemption where Mel's desserts are involved.'

She laughed, saw his eyes flash, and her heart flipped at the message they conveyed, causing her to blurt out the first words that came to mind.

'You look fit and toned. Do you exercise regularly?'

His lips curled into a knowing smile and heat flooded her cheeks. She'd admitted to noticing his physique. His light chuckle sent tingles down her spine and ignited heat coils in her belly. If she closed her eyes she'd be able to count the Outback stars in the image the sound generated. She fought the impulse, keeping them locked with his amused gaze.

'I have a few weights at home and I swim and surf most of the year. Plus our frequent family picnic or barbecue get-togethers always include team games resulting in friendly riots. Never missed unless I'm interstate.'

That pang hit again. Family gatherings involved genuine hugs, kisses and lots of fun and laughter. She'd had those with Mum and although her friends' families had been sincere in their affections, it just wasn't quite the same as actually being related.

'Cassie?'

She blinked, looked across the table into caring green eyes and came back to the moment.

'I'm trying to picture a gathering of all the close relations Mel says you have. How do you keep track of birthdays and anniversaries?'

He shrugged and the sticky moment passed. 'Computer calendar, and a great-aunt who never forgets and keeps everyone up to date.'

The waitress returned with a bottle of Chardonnay, and he nodded his approval.

'That's fine, thank you, no need for tasting.'

Once the bottle was in the ice bucket stand and they were alone, he raised his glass and quirked an eyebrow.

'Any special toast you'd like to drink to?'

'To Mel, enjoying the fun of discovering forgotten treasured mementoes, and staying in the home where she's been so happy for many more years.'

Jack froze. He couldn't think of anything better, though having Cassie in his arms again came close. This time ending with a kiss he wouldn't be pulling back from as he had this morning.

He was surprised to see the liquid in his glass rippling from the trembling of his hand. Cassie's was steady as a rock as she completed the ritual then sipped her wine. Watching the slight movement in her throat, he imagined her pulse accelerating under his lips as he pressed them to her delicate skin. The tip of her tongue licked a stray drop of wine from her lower lip and *his* pulse shot to the sky.

Get to know her, huh.

Forget life and history. He wanted to taste the sweetness of a fervent kiss, feel her yield to his caressing hands. Memorise her uninhibited sounds as they made love.

He gulped a mouthful of wine, silently sending an apology to the maker for the insult. By focusing on the crisp cool flavour as it slid down his throat, he regained some inner semblance of restraint.

'Would you rather have a beer?' Cassie's concerned tone deepened his guilt.

'No, forgive my lapse in manners. Wine is my preferred choice when dining with a beautiful woman.'

Her burst of natural laughter undid the calming effort in one second flat. Every cell in his body responded to her musical delight.

'That, Jackson Randell, is an old cliché unworthy of a modern gentleman.'

Her imitation of his aunt left him both flabbergasted and elated. His airway seized up, immobilised by a clear view of her slender neck as she proudly lifted her chin, the sparkle in her eyes and the unintended invitation of her parted lips.

This teasing aspect of her nature was a revelation, one he'd like to explore at leisure. And encourage every chance he got. When he finally managed to draw breath, he pointed his finger at her and feigned a sombre expression.

'The reason they are clichés is because they are so often true.'

For a split second he saw the sparkle dim. Before he could confirm it, she broke eye contact as the waitress appeared with bread rolls.

Jack could see the slight furrow of her brow. It seemed she didn't agree with or hadn't liked his last remark. He'd meant it as light-hearted banter. Had she taken it as flirting?

Her face lit up as she selected a roll for her side plate. 'Ooh, they're warm and smell fresh baked. And thank you for the compliment.'

'Your expression disagreed.'

'A flashback from the past. I once dated someone who frequently quoted for effect without feeling the sentiment. For me sincerity is as important as honesty.'

'If I say it, I mean it.' His eyes were drawn to her neat white teeth as she bit into her roll, and he felt a surge of desire as the tip of her tongue licked away a few stray crumbs from her tempting lips.

'Mmm, a small touch yet it makes the meal special.'

Struggling for normality, he leant back in his seat. 'Have you always lived in Adelaide?' He immediately regretted his brusque tone.

Cassie stopped chewing, forced herself to swallow. *The start of the get-to-know-you quiz.*

Was she ready? Would she ever be with this charismatic man who could charm secrets from a clam? She met his steady gaze, surprised to see a shade of remorse in the usually clear green eyes.

'Yes. I enjoyed school and have friendships that date back to my first year in secondary. They, and Mum's friends, were my lifeline when her cancer was diagnosed. Without them, I'd have been lost.'

His brow creased and his eyes narrowed as if he found difficulty in visualising life without all his relatives. 'And there's really no other family?'

'Mum's sister lived overseas and we lost contact years ago.' Not the full answer. Not a lie.

'Wanna share mine? There's a few I'll willingly farm off at times.'

The mood lightened with his teasing remark. Their laughter mingled and it was the nicest sound she'd heard in a long time, sparking a warm glow in her abdomen that radiated to her fingertips and toes.

'Do I get to choose?'

'Only from the ones *I* select.' The inflection in his tone and the gleam in his eyes suggested none would be young, handsome males.

The arrival of their entrées, chicken wings with small side salad for her and ravioli for him, deferred talk for the moment. When the waitress reached for the wine to top their glasses up, Jack drank the remainder in his before nodding and allowing her to proceed.

Cassie's perplexity must have shown because Jack explained his action.

'If it's refilled from empty I can keep track of how much I drink. I don't claim to have always been that smart but I've never driven if there's the slightest chance I might be over the limit. Learnt an early lesson.'

'You had an accident?'

'A close call when a car shot out at speed in front of my cousin on our way home after pizza dinner out with friends. He'd had two beers spaced through the evening. Even one more might have slowed his reactions and it could have been a lot worse.'

Her fingers stilled on her cutlery. She froze, wanting to cover her ears and not hear the rest.

'John swung left and the guy veered enough to sideswipe the bonnet and spin us round. Apart from almost writing off both cars, the other driver spent a week in hospital, and lost his licence for a year. We four ended up with minor injuries and bruises. It was… Cassie?'

When she didn't react, he reached over to cover her hand with his. She started, blinked and gave a quick shake of her head.

'You've gone pale. Have I stirred up a bad memory? You should have stopped me.'

She stared at his worried expression for a moment then down at their joined hands and took a shuddering breath.

'No, I imagined you... A silly notion. I'm fine, really.'

He trailed his fingers along hers as he withdrew his hand, as if reluctant to break the physical connection. She regretted the loss of his comforting touch, almost twisted her hand to keep it there. Almost.

Picking up her knife and fork, she concentrated on her food. She hadn't expected the answer to her casual question to have such a profound effect on her. As he'd spoken, images sprang into her mind—Jack helpless as the car bore down on them. Jack hurt and bleeding, in pain, waiting for help.

Why had her imagination suddenly burst into full force? Why not when she'd struggled to write essays for her English classes? And why had she ordered chicken wings, which were so awkward and messy to eat with cutlery?

'Use your fingers, Cassie. It's allowed.'

Her head jerked up and her heart skipped more than a beat at the playful look in his eyes and his warm smile. She stole a furtive glance around the room. No one was looking their way except the waitress returning with a finger bowl of warm water.

Reassured, she chose a wing and took a bite. It was delicious and spicy, tingling her tastebuds. If the main was as flavoursome, and they avoided controversial subjects, she'd have no regrets at the end of the evening.

Jack watched Cassie's colour return, wished she'd finished her sentence. It didn't take much nous to work it out, though. He wavered between liking the rush of satisfaction that she'd cared about him being injured, and concern at the knowledge she might.

'Have you travelled much, Cassie?'

Her smile proved he'd chosen an acceptable topic. You

couldn't get more uncontroversial than holidays, and people's choices revealed a lot more than they realised.

'The eastern states during school or work breaks. One trip to New Zealand with Mum and another with two friends for a wedding. We hired a car and stayed for two weeks. I'd love to travel through Greece and Italy.'

'Not the bright lights and night life of London or New York?'

She had his total concentration; his elbows were on the table, fingers locked and his chin resting on his thumbs. Everyone else in the room faded, their voices becoming a muted background hum.

'To me they're pretty much like any capital city in Australia, apart from iconic features. It won't happen often, so I want to experience something new and completely different to what I'd find here.'

'True, you…' He straightened up as a group of new arrivals were ushered past their table.

Cassie spoke before he could continue. 'This place is a good example, another reason for avoiding popular western cities. Why fly hundreds of miles to eat familiar meals in similar establishments to those in your own suburbs? If I'm going to spend big money on air fares and accommodation I want to try true local cuisine.'

'I agree. When you do, remember that in many places abroad local cuisine is tailored to suit western palates.'

He'd bet the value of his treasured ute she didn't realise how much her body language and expressive eyes revealed.

The sharp wrench to his gut earlier when he'd called her out of her daydream added to his growing certainty that she still mourned the loss of her mother. In the seconds she'd taken to blink and refocus, he'd seen deep-seated sorrow in her lovely brown eyes.

Don't go soft. His main objective was to protect Mel.

Involvement with the beguiling woman facing him across the table could mean pain for any one of the three.

She dipped her fingers in the bowl, wiped them on her serviette then pushed her plate to the side. Leaning forward, arms on the table, she gave him a smile that generated a heatwave in his stomach. It was like hot coffee on a cold morning, hitting the spot then spreading throughout the body. A perfect awakening any morning.

'I take it the wings and salad were as tasty as they looked.'

'The best I've had for ages.' After sipping her wine, she tilted her head, just a tad, a very beguiling action.

'Do you enjoy gardening or is it a labour of love for Mel? The lawns and vegetable plots are large for a city dwelling.'

Shoot, she was good. If he didn't get his act together, she'd be the one going home with all the knowledge and he'd have learnt little about her.

'It's part of the maintenance side of my business, which I admit I find therapeutic. There's also the added bonus of fresh harvested fruit and veggies—beats store bought any day. As kids we grew up picking and eating whatever was ripe at the time, and I'm especially partial to peaches, oranges and apricots.' And since yesterday their scent on soft pink-tinged skin.

'You don't grow your own?'

'No, out back I have a small lawn and border; the front's landscaped with shrubs and stones. How about you?'

'We have miniature lemon, apricot and mandarin trees, plus whatever anyone gets the whim to plant in the cleared area.' She looked behind him. 'Here come our mains. Let's see if their vegetables taste as good as our home grown.'

They chatted about movies, favourite Australian tourist spots they'd visited and Jack's parents' home about twenty kilometres from Brisbane's city centre. He made her laugh with tales of trekking to the top end of Queensland.

* * *

Cassie didn't want the meal to end. Jack had sampled her barramundi and given her a taste of his steak. Sumptuous setting, scrumptious meal. Charming and attentive company.

After a meticulous perusal of the dessert menu, she laid it on the table with a heartfelt sigh. 'They all sound scrumptious, and if I wasn't so full I'd be tempted to try one.'

'Maybe next time. Would you like to go for a walk and have coffee?'

Her heartbeat fluttered and she tingled all over. He wanted to extend the evening, *and* repeat their shared experience some time. Keeping her voice normal and level took effort.

'Hot chocolate would be a great way to round off the evening.'

Cassie more than liked the way Jack helped her into her jacket. The protective arm he put around her as they crossed the street somehow became a handhold that felt warm and protective. They strolled along, checking every open venue. Finally selected a quiet café near the hill leading down to the city.

She hid a grin when he asked for extra marshmallows in her hot chocolate and ordered black tea for himself, claiming her choice was too sweet for him. They took a table for two by the window and watched the passing parade of people enjoying a night out.

Hers was coming to an end and she'd have to face the crucial decision. If he tried to kiss her when he took her home, did she let him? Did she want him to? What if he made no attempt, just said a polite goodnight? That last thought was surprisingly depressing.

'They must be freezing.' Jack's voice held a hint of amusement as he stared through the glass at three girls in form-fitting tops, short skirts and ultra high-heeled shoes. Stunningly made-up, they drew the attention of every male they passed as they headed for one of the popular night spots in the area.

Cassie laughed. 'At that age you're immune to the weather, especially when you're about to enter a room full of eager, available young men.'

She envied them their confidence and poise, and wished them success in their search for their special man. Hers was still out there somewhere, hopefully looking for her.

CHAPTER EIGHT

JACK SEEMED LOST in thought on the drive home, or perhaps he'd run out of conversation. Her gaze kept straying to his hands on the wheel, noting their firm competent control. Her stomach clenched as she recalled his long, strong fingers when he'd assisted her into and out of this vehicle, and on her waist as they'd danced. Her palm tingled at the recollection of his workman's palm on her lotion-smoothed soft skin as he'd clasped their joined hands to his chest.

As the familiar music and lyrics played in her mind, she closed her eyes and leant back onto the headrest. The quiet rhythm of the ute's engine seemed to be part of the orchestral sound.

'Tired, Cassie?' Jack's resonant voice penetrated her dreamy haze.

By the time she languidly opened her eyes, his head was facing forward. She caught back the sigh that rose in her throat at his striking profile.

'A little. Thank you for inviting me out tonight, Jack. I'm glad I accepted.'

'My pleasure. I guess you'll be sleeping in tomorrow.' She heard a hitch in his voice, a growing edginess as he spoke, and couldn't think of a reason.

'Maybe. I'll have to do the chores I'd planned for Friday.'

'Leave them. Treat it as a bonus day and relax. Do something for yourself that you've been putting off. When's your next job?'

'Monday, all next week over near the plaza. A ten-minute drive from home.'

* * *

Jack's fingers involuntarily tightened on the wheel. Growling internally, he forced them to relax. They'd met about thirty hours ago; no way should he be affected by the prospect of not seeing her for a week.

'You'll be at Mel's on Friday?' They were a few blocks from her home, not much time left to talk.

'Yes, to finalise what we've done and arrange another session if she still wants to proceed. Having two days to think it over might have made her reconsider. Even staggered full clean-outs can be daunting.'

'Much as I hate any reminder that she's getting older, I have to concede it will ease her mind. Won't stop the idea of her not being in that house tearing me apart.'

'She'll be around for a long time yet, Jack.'

In his peripheral vision he saw her hand lift towards him, and his heartbeat rose then fell when it dropped back into her lap. She'd reached out in comfort, changed her mind, and the depth of his disappointment shook him.

He drove into her driveway, ignoring the empty space in the street. Parking there meant walking her to her door and, seeing she'd come out to meet him earlier, he figured she'd prefer he didn't.

'Hang on, I'll come round.'

He couldn't resist lifting her from the cab, allowing his hands to linger on her waist, and pulling her a little closer before setting her on the ground. He basked in the warmth of her sweet grateful smile before releasing her and stepping back.

She looked tired and there'd be no goodnight kiss, not even quick and gentle, much as he wanted to feel the softness of her lips under his.

'Thank you, Jack. I had a...memorable evening.'

'Me too. Sleep well and enjoy tomorrow. If the timing's right, I'll see you Friday afternoon.'

Was it hope that flared in her stunning brown eyes? And what word had she bitten back?

He closed the door and kept his arm around her until they were at the driver's side of the bonnet. Fighting the desire storming through him, he caressed a gentle path down her cheek and cupped her chin with his fingers. Wasn't sure how he kept his voice steady. Or stopped himself from pressing a gentle kiss on her lips, which were slightly parted and so inviting.

'Sweet dreams, Cassie. I'll wait until you're inside.'

She hesitated for a second before uttering a husky, 'Goodnight, Jack,' and turning towards the house. He watched every graceful step, curling his left hand's fingers on his thigh as she unlocked the door and disappeared inside. Was she describing her evening as memorable to whoever was waiting in the front room?

The tautness in Jack's muscles began to ease while he was waiting at a red traffic light two blocks away. He'd been a hair's-breadth from wrapping her in his arms and finding out if she tasted as sweet as he imagined. Might have, if he hadn't seen the glow from the television.

He'd proved once that his lack of control could lead to tragedy. Letting someone get close meant letting your guard down, revealing your emotions, allowing theirs to sway you against your better judgement.

He hadn't lost his temper since Tara had died, never allowed any situation to get out of hand. And he avoided women who used cold shoulder treatment or flirting to get their own way. Keeping his true assets secret discouraged attention from those who favoured wealthy men.

Cassie was different. He sensed she'd compromise and placate rather than inflame. Knowing he came from an affluent family seemed to discourage her from closer contact. He slid a USB into the port, hoping the Guns N' Roses soundtrack would distract him. Didn't work.

Sunlight creeping around the edges of her blinds woke Cassie without help from her alarm. So much for predicted rain. She felt loose and relaxed as she did a slow leisurely stretch plus a few neck circles.

Had she dreamt of Jack? Couldn't remember. She'd slept deep and sound, from the moment she'd snuggled under her quilt and closed her eyes. His suggestion popped into her head, making her smile. A bonus day, for special treats. Infinitely better than washing clothes and cleaning the bathroom.

Grabbing her phone, she scrolled to Narelle. Her best friend's young son spent Thursday with his grandma so with luck she'd be free. No answer so she left a message suggesting they meet for lunch and window-shopping therapy. Rolling onto her side to return the mobile to her bedside cabinet, she gazed at the framed picture there and smiled.

'You'd have liked him, Mum. Open and direct. Doesn't hide his disapproval but is ready to hear another opinion and admit he might be wrong. Not the man for me, though. But then I'm not sure there is one I could completely trust and confide in.'

She threw back the covers, and shivered when her bare feet landed on the cold lino. Perhaps carpeting her bedroom should be shifted from third on her to-do list to top. Unless spring warmth arrived early this year.

A short hot shower brightened her up, and the heady aroma from the coffee percolator drew her to the kitchen and Phil, a cheerful early riser.

'Hi, stranger.' Phil put her special mug next to the one already on the bench. 'You're not due back till tonight.'

Taking two slices of bread from the packet, she set them

to toast. 'Sorry, I forgot to change the chart last night when I came home to change. I'm going back to Woodcroft tomorrow for one day, not sure when I'll be back.'

The chart the three housemates had devised kept track of when they'd be home and the division of chores. Even allowing for the occasional lapse, it had worked well for them for over three years.

'Hitch in the job? It's a long drive for a day's work.'

'Unavoidable, and the lady might have more for me to do in the next few weeks. Brad home?'

'He left before sun-up.' He placed her steaming drink on the table and sat down with his. 'What's your plan for the weekend?'

Narelle's call came as they talked and, after arranging their meeting, she passed the phone to Phil while she cleared the table.

'Barbecue with the gang on Sunday,' he told her as he put her mobile down and took his mug and plate to the sink. 'See you later.'

Her mobile rang again as she walked back to her bedroom. *Jack.*

'Hi, Cassie, sleep well?'

'Very. Thank you for calling, and again for last night.'

'Just checking. You have a relaxing day.'

'I will. I'm having lunch with a friend.'

'Good. I'll see you tomorrow, Cassie.'

'Mmm, tomorrow.'

She disconnected and cradled her phone in her palm, staring at his ID. Why had he called, and why had her brain gone missing? Because it had been occupied with drying her throat, ranking up her heartbeat and prickling all her nerve endings.

Narelle's blonde hair with green highlights and her flair for colourful fashions made her easy to spot in the spacious food court of the shopping centre. Salad wraps and milk-shakes were on the table.

They chatted about friends, Narelle's progressing second pregnancy and the challenges of rearing an active three-year-old boy. Laughing off his latest escapade, her astute friend pushed her plate away and studied Cassie with questioning eyes.

'So, give. I can't quite pick it but something's happened. You have an aura about you.'

Her emotions showed? How the heck could Cassie say she was attracted to a charismatic man who was very protective of her employer, his great-aunt? And that the desire, even if merely physical on his part, was reciprocated. Hey, wasn't that what it was for her?

'Cassie Clarkson, you're blushing.'

'I'm not. I was thinking.'

'About who?'

About how to describe the last two days with drastic editing.

'The house is similar to the historic one you considered buying when you got married, beautifully maintained and furnished. Mel is friendly, down-to-earth and well on the way to full recovery after a car accident.'

She drank through her straw, gaining time to formulate the right words.

'And she has this great-nephew who—get that match-making look off your face, Narelle—is handsome, charming and so out of my league I'm surprised we speak the same language.'

'Handsome as in to-die-for?'

Mesmerising dark green eyes, finger-itching unruly brown hair and a tempting full mouth. Add to the mix that haunting crackle of a laugh...

'With a smile on your lips.' Removing the straw, Cassie emptied her glass. 'Let's go and challenge my bank card.'

Yet even as she placed the food wrappers in the bin she was thinking of Jack rather than the clothes she was about to try on. Was he having lunch with Mel right now or mowing the lawns he'd postponed yesterday?

At roughly the same time as Cassie used her credit card for the third time, Jack drove into Mel's driveway. He'd barely hit the bed before he'd fallen asleep last night, and had spent today recalling Cassie's revelations. He'd learned a lot about how she responded to words and actions, yet little of her life or history.

He wasn't sure why he'd called her this morning. To hear her voice and find out how she'd slept? To ask what she had planned because the sunshine meant he'd be working not far from her most of the day? Whatever he'd intended, her response meant he'd spent the day pondering whether her friend was male or female.

Sam greeted him as he walked in the back door, and Mel was in the family room rearranging footwear. He hugged and kissed her, held on a little longer than usual. Hated having to accept the realities that ageing brought.

'You look tired, Jack. Another late night?'

'No, a very pleasant one, actually.' He kept the details to himself because she might ask why, and he had no plausible answer. 'Did you really wear every one of these shoes?'

'I must have. Coffee and scones?'

'Tea, and I'll get it. I've had a few ideas I want to discuss with you about the house.'

Her face clouded for a moment. 'So have I. It's all so confusing but better to have everything worked out now rather than the family having to deal with it.'

He drew her back into his arms. 'We'll all do whatever you feel most comfortable with, Mel. Your peace of mind is top priority.'

She tapped his cheek, as she'd done hundreds of times over the years, smiled and pulled away.

'I'm reasonably healthy, my leg is much better and I can still cook up a feast. Go pop the scones in the oven for a few minutes. The jam and cream are in the fridge.'

'Do you want any of those shoes taken upstairs?'

'No, Cassie will check them off on her list first.'

Cassie. Tomorrow. And soon for a week at a time.

By then he'd better have worked out how he was going to handle this magnetism between them.

The electric jug was boiling and Mel's homemade biscuits were fresh from the oven when Cassie arrived on Friday morning. They sat in the lounge and, after she'd heard about the trip to Murray Bridge, discussed the day's agenda.

'The clothes and shoes are sorted and ready for the final tick-off. Jack and I phoned everyone and the women are coming Sunday afternoon to take their pick. The men and children will be here for a barbecue later.'

Cassie thought of the wide veranda along the back of the house packed full of people enjoying each other's company, laughing, joking and telling stories. For a moment the injustice of fate twisted her heart and her fingers curled into her palms. She was grateful Mum's suffering had been short, but sometimes couldn't help but be angry she'd lost her too soon.

Blinking away threatening tears, she turned her head and found herself staring at Mel and Bob's wedding photo. What were Jack's words? *'Imagine losing someone after forty-five years.'* More if you counted the courtship.

Yet the woman opposite her had overcome her despair, and was winning the battle against physical pain and loss of independence, buoyed by family support. Cassie accepted that growing up with no other relatives but Mum had influenced her view on life. Her friends and their families had proved she need never feel alone, yet sometimes she couldn't escape the void.

She knew she had so much to be thankful for. Shaking away the blue feeling, she helped herself to another honey and almond biscuit.

'Better hope for sunshine. Will they all fit on the veranda?'

'Out there, in here and in the family room, depending on whether you want to talk sport, gossip or play hide and seek.'

'You have a wonderful house and garden for children to play in.'

'My home is what I need to think about.'

It was the kind of mixed feelings day that left Cassie drained by the time she got home around four after being held up three times by roadworks. Knowing she was partly to blame, well, mostly to be truthful, for her high expectations of seeing Jack didn't help. Neither did telling herself she'd lived twenty-seven years without his presence so what was the big deal about not seeing him for ten days.

He'd made a quick call mid-afternoon to tell his aunt he'd been held up and would pop in tomorrow. Hadn't asked about her or to speak to her, which hurt a little though the conversation barely lasted two minutes so he must have been in a hurry. She could also understand he might want to keep last night's dinner a secret from his family.

She took a long hot shower, something she rarely did, trying to lather away her blues. Dressed in warm trousers, a thick bright green patterned jumper and her favourite mood-picking-up red boots, she studied the contents of the larder and refrigerator. Nothing there tempted her appetite.

Two phone calls, a 'Fancy eating at the pub tonight?' greeting to Phil when he arrived home, and the evening had been arranged. Just what she needed. A packed room,

Aussie rules football on the wall-mounted televisions and enough chatter to stop her thinking. The food might not be as fancy as Wednesday night but it was always fresh and tasty.

CHAPTER NINE

THEY ENDED UP in the overflow dining area next to the poker machine room. Sipping her Malibu and lemonade, she joined in a spirited debate on the current football finals. If someone hadn't tapped her on the shoulder and pointed to her handbag under the table, she'd have missed her ringtone.

It had stopped by the time she'd pulled her mobile out. Sliding it open, she saw Jack's caller ID and went into the quieter entrance. There was no reason for the uplift in her spirits, or for her pulse to race. Probably just a query on next week's agenda.

'Cassie.' She heard the smile in his voice, which rekindled heat in her abdomen, scary yet exciting. Seeking more privacy, she stepped outside, sheltering under a canopy.

'Hi, I'm sorry I missed your call. It's kinda noisy here.'

'I can hear it. Quite a crowd you've got there.' Did she imagine the slight bite of disapproval in his tone?

'I had a rotten drive home, and didn't feel like cooking. Called some friends and we met at the pub for dinner. Didn't realise it would be so busy, but it's fun.' She knew she was babbling, tried a different topic.

'Have you seen Mel today?' There were traffic sounds in the background so he wasn't at home.

'No, I spoke to her earlier. The quick repair job I'd planned turned into an all-dayer.'

'You're not driving now?' *Idiot*. She heard the concern in her voice, hoped it didn't transmit down the line.

'No. But it's nice to know you care, Cassie.' It must have. 'I prefer to pull over and talk, keep hands-free for necessities. I've stopped to pick up Chinese takeaway.' It sounded as if he was clearing his throat. 'I thought about you today.'

Their talk was a continuation of her day, emotions shooting up and down, uncertainty fogging her normal comprehension. Answering with the truth wasn't an option. She dredged her mind for a light, harmless answer. *Ditto* came to mind, discarded as too clichéd.

'The correct reply is I thought of you too.'

Now he was laughing at her. Or with her? Either way, she liked the intimacy he managed to instil into his resonant voice. She could play the flirting game too, over the line, where she was safe from his compelling green eyes, intoxicating touch and seductive lips.

'Are you fishing for compliments, Jack Randell?'

Even across the expanse of a major city and using a mobile phone didn't diminish the power of his crackling laugh. She could almost feel the heat from the campfire and hear the rustle of spinifex being blown across the sand.

'Not until I can see you and tell if you mean it. Wanna do FaceTime?'

'No.'

'Are you blushing, Cassie?'

How the heck could he tell? 'Why would I be? We're just talking?'

'I can hear it in your voice.'

It was her turn to chuckle. 'You're full of it, Jack Randell. You should be selling stuff, not repairing it.'

'Pity *you're* not buying.' His voice deepened as he emphasised the second word, sending quivers shooting up and down her spine. What effect would he have on her if they were together? The very thought robbed her of breath and coherent reasoning.

Thankfully, she heard his name called in the background, saving her from replying, giving her seconds to regroup.

'My order's ready.'

'You'd better go. Enjoy your exotic meal, Jack.'

'Don't have too much fun, Cassie. Sweet dreams.'

'Goodnight.' She stayed outside, inhaling and exhaling slowly and steadily. How could she stay immune to the charisma of a man who could turn her inside out over the phone?

Jack accepted his carry bag of hot foil containers and strode out of his favourite Chinese restaurant. He'd ordered two mains and a special fried rice—wished it were more, and that Cassie was joining him to eat.

Who was 'we'? Did it involve the same person she'd met for lunch yesterday? Tossing his dinner onto the passenger seat, he slid into his ute and was buckling in when he became aware he was grinning.

Cassie had been flirting. Bet she wouldn't next time they met. There'd be no safety of distance between them. The idea of provoking her, and seeing her creamy cheeks blush rosy red, was appealing. Tracing a slow fingertip path across her skin to her chin even more so. Especially if it led to him tilting her head and covering her irresistible lips with his.

His libido was driving his imagination again, a problem he'd been having since mid-afternoon Tuesday. Only three days ago, but it seemed like a lifetime.

He ate in his dimmed lounge, feet on the coffee table as he watched a documentary on distant solar systems. For the first time since he'd moved in, he was conscious of the space around him and the absence of any other person's presence apart from numerous family photos in the downstairs rooms.

That was the way he wanted it, right? No permanent housemate disturbing his peace, no one else's belongings lying around or cluttering his bathroom, and no annoying habits to trigger his temper. No fights, no repercussions. No more regrets.

He'd had family and friends for short visits but, since moving in two years ago, he'd never had a woman stay overnight. Had rarely taken anyone upstairs to his bedroom, preferring to keep any intimacy in their homes. His stormy relationship with Tara had far-reaching consequences.

Her statement that she intended to marry a rich man had amused him when they'd met at nineteen. As they'd dated, her craving for attention from him and other men, and her sense of entitlement for anything she took a fancy to, had become tedious. The fights had grown more bitter until that last tragic time when he'd turned his back and let her walk out.

At her funeral, guilt and pain had strengthened his vow to avoid that type of woman, no matter how beautiful, and never, ever lose his temper, no matter what the provocation.

Why did the strict control he maintained on his mind and body slip away whenever he saw, spoke to, even thought about Cassie Clarkson? He had no idea when he would next see her. From Monday, she'd be with her next client.

She and Mel had pencilled in the following week for her to come to Woodcroft. For him, it suddenly seemed like the long wait for Christmas morning.

Gathering up the leftovers and his empty beer bottle, he headed for the kitchen. Once the trash was in the bin, bottle in recycle and the coffee table wiped over, he sprawled on the settee with a finance report. Had to read it twice to take anything in.

After less than two and a half days with her new employers Cassie found herself wishing for an early end to the project, a very unusual occurrence for her. She couldn't help comparing the semi-retired couple with most of her other clients.

While they were friendly enough towards *her*, the air of discord between husband and wife affected her normal relaxed manner. There'd been no warning signs when she'd come to quote on the assignment. It was becoming clear that very little from their overcrowded home would be sold or given away, and she'd bet they'd still be here years from now, each blaming the other for the lack of space.

The *ding* alerting her to an incoming text was a welcome diversion. Her pulse tripped at the call sign. *Jack*.

Call me when you are free. Only need a few minutes.

She called immediately, realising the second his phone began to ring that this might seem too eager. Too late to hang up now.

'I caught you on a break, huh?'

Not from her body's reaction to the sound of him, or from his image flashing into her mind. It had been four days and seventeen hours since she'd heard his voice.

But who's counting?

'A quick one. Is there something you need?' Was it her imagination or did he groan? His reply was definitely gravel-rough.

'Are you free to have dinner with Mel and me in the city tonight? She'd like to talk to you.'

'I'm free but…'

'Good. Take a taxi and I'll reimburse you. We'll drive you home.'

'I'll catch an O-Bahn bus, much quicker from home than in traffic.'

'I'd rather you—'

'Gotta go. Where have you booked?' Taxis were an indulgence for special occasions or emergencies, though his protective attitude was endearing. It wouldn't have surprised her if he'd offered to pick her up.

There was a pained silence for a moment. His disgruntled throaty rumble was followed by the name and address of the restaurant. 'I'm looking forward to seeing you, Cassie,' he replied to her thanks in his gravelly voice, leaving her with a racing heartbeat and trembling knees.

She spent the rest of the day pondering the purpose of the meeting while automatically typing lists for her clients. What had changed and why couldn't it wait until she arrived in Woodcroft on Monday? And why the two of them?

Selecting what to wear to the classy city hotel that evening was another worry. Her new red dress was out, already worn. She finally settled on mid-grey trousers and a new matching sleeveless buttoned top over a dark blue blouse. Her long black boots would keep her legs warm and weren't too high for the two short walks ahead.

Spinning away from the image in the mirror, she slipped on her winter coat, picked up her handbag, and huffed. She'd never been concerned what people thought of her clothes or status in life, was proud of the woman she was because of Mum's guidance. But then she'd never been wined and dined by the upper echelon of Adelaide until last week.

Cassie arrived at the venue two minutes early, and was told her hosts were already seated. She was escorted to their round table adjacent to the balcony, and Mel's open arms drew her into a hug. She instinctively answered with a soft kiss on her hostess's cheek then moved round to where the maître d' waited, holding her chair.

As she sat, her foot touched Jack's stretched out leg under the table. He made no acknowledgement so, thankfully, he mustn't have felt anything. The glow of his welcoming smile sparked a fire in her belly, spreading heat along her veins, and she couldn't control the delicious vibration that followed. He and Mel already had pre-dinner drinks. She declined, thanked the waiter who filled her water glass and took a soothing mouthful.

'You look beautiful, Cassie. Thank you for coming.' Jack raised his glass in salute, and any cooling effects from the icy liquid were instantly negated by the burning admiration in his dark green eyes.

She looked the same as last Wednesday, so how had she evolved from nice to beautiful?

'I concur,' Mel chipped in. 'I'd love to have worn some of the fashions around today when I was young.'

'From what I've been told, you were right at the forefront of whatever was trendy, Mel.' Jack tipped his glass towards her. 'And photos I've seen show you carried it with flair.'

'Flatterer.' Mel tapped his hand, and they grinned at each other. 'Now, I hope you don't mind, Cassie, we've already ordered a bottle of Semillon. It's my favourite with fish and I fancy the grilled whiting tonight.'

The menu choices were comprehensible so why didn't Cassie's brain process them? Could it be the tantalising aroma of an exotic cologne teasing her nostrils, and the brush of an ankle against hers, stirring her blood? She daren't meet Jack's gaze, found it hard to breathe, and gave a husky response to the waiter's offer of wine.

She sipped the pleasantly crisp-tasting Semillon as they discussed starters, wishing she had a better knowledge of South Australian grown wines. The consensus was for a shared dip plate entrée; Jack ordered salmon, and Cassie veal scaloppine.

She handed her menu to the waiter, reassembled her jumbled thoughts and spoke to Mel. Sensing Jack's intensity, she forced a light, casual tone. 'I appreciate being invited to dinner, and I'm sure I'll enjoy every course, but *why* am I here?'

Mel answered. 'My granddaughter's husband phoned

this morning. The specialist is concerned about the baby's growth so she's admitted Janette for monitoring, and mentioned the possibility of being induced. Janette's asked if I'll go over, though I'm not sure how much help I'll be.'

'Immeasurable, just by being there,' Cassie said. Her indomitable presence and optimistic outlook on life made her the heart and spirit of every generation of the family. Cassie knew because she'd lost the one who'd provided that essence for her.

Jack made a silent vow to thank Cassie for her insight when they were alone. As he covered his aunt's hand with his and squeezed, endorsing those few accurate words, he smiled at Cassie, letting her see his gratitude.

'Cassie's right, Mel. We don't acknowledge it enough but we all depend on your help and advice.'

Mel's eyes glistened with emotion and he swore never to take her being there for granted again.

'And my baking.'

They all laughed, though he noticed Cassie's lips didn't quite make a full smile. The sparkle in her eyes had dimmed.

'So you'd like to postpone our arrangement. Not a problem. We can reschedule once you're home.' Matter-of-fact tone. Business mode.

He couldn't fathom the reason for her sudden mood change. She'd told them postponements weren't unusual so why…? Without warning, his heartbeat revved up and anticipation surged. Could it be because any delay meant not seeing him? That sounded egotistical but there was no denying the attraction between them.

He concentrated on Cassie's face for her reaction as Mel explained.

'Not exactly, dear. I'd just like to alter the conditions. Would you consider house-sitting for me, and doing an inventory of each room while you're there?'

It was like watching a flame flicker into life as Cassie's eyes widened in surprise then glowed. She made no sound. Her lips opened, forming a perfect O, and her fingers slipped down the stem of her wineglass and fanned out on the white tablecloth. He imagined them splaying across his chest as he covered her tempting lips with his mouth.

'Are you sure? There must be a family member who'd be happy to move in while you're away. I'd never even stayed overnight on a job until you invited me.'

She was so delightfully bemused, he ached to take her in his arms and reassure her. His own instant elated response had surprised him, made him re-examine his attitude. Cassie's appeal was different to any woman he'd known but his vow to never form a lasting relationship was absolute. She might not judge a man by his financial standing but proximity could reveal faults and weaknesses.

His aunt's proposal included him calling in regularly to give her support, day-to-day domestic contact when true character couldn't be suppressed for long. But he'd kept his quick temper under control for nine years, wouldn't risk losing it ever again.

'No one's available at such short notice,' Mel replied. 'You've already allocated me next week, and I won't be a distraction while you work. If you have to leave for your next contract, Jack will arrange something.'

Cassie turned towards him and he gave her an encouraging smile.

'It'll be similar to your normal life, except listing and living will be in the same building, and you'll be dog-minding as well. Plus there's the added attraction of me being available any time you need help.'

He arched his eyebrows in an attempt to make her laugh and succeeded. That was when he realised how much he'd missed the rippling effect her musical sound created in his body.

Their dips and assorted breads arrived and, as they sampled and compared tastes, they discussed Cassie's moving in and the order of rooms to be inventoried. Jack sensed Cassie's enthusiasm overrode her apprehension. She really loved the career she'd chosen.

His career was about to veer onto the new path he'd planned from the beginning. The downside was that suits and corporate meetings would inevitably replace hands-on repairs and maintenance. But he'd willingly keep doing handyman jobs for Mel and his family.

'My sister Val is travelling with Mel tomorrow; she's happy for any excuse to catch up with relatives, and shop in Melbourne. Sam can come with me until you move in.'

'I'll finish my current job late Friday morning.' Her eyes met his, now bright and shiny, open and honest. 'Should be able to leave home mid-afternoon.'

'I'll arrange my work so I can meet you at the house with the keys. Call me when you're ready to head off.'

He topped up the women's wine, the residue making up his limit for driving. Now the main objective of the evening had been accomplished, he could devote his time to entertaining them.

He cajoled both of them into ordering rich calorie-laden desserts, claiming he couldn't resist and he'd feel guilty eating alone in front of them. And emphatically dismissed Cassie's suggestion she take a taxi home.

'I'd be scolded all the way home if I allowed it. Apart from being ingrained behaviour—' he grinned at Mel '—it'll be my pleasure.' Arching an eyebrow, he reminded Cassie of his statement when he'd invited her out before.

Cassie conceded to his request, or rather insistence, with a smile. When he went to fetch his ute, she complimented his good manners.

'I'll admit to enjoying being spoilt and cosseted occasionally. Especially so smoothly.'

Especially by Jack.

Mel laughed. 'Doesn't every woman? I've always tried to instil respect for others in the younger generation. Some of the boys were more challenging than others, but thankfully they finally matured.' She gave a beaming smile. 'I'm proud of each and every one of them.'

She didn't need to state the obvious but it was what she hadn't said that interested Cassie. How *bad boy* had Jack been, and what had caused him to re-evaluate his life?

CHAPTER TEN

CASSIE CLIMBED INTO the driver's side of the rear bench seat as Jack helped his aunt up into the front of his ute. Her fingertips twitched with longing to smooth his unruly brown hair, within her reach. Closing her eyes, she pictured his suntanned, work-rough hands, so competent on the wheel, so heart-stopping when he touched her.

She slipped into a dream world of physical contact, those first *zings* over her skin, his lean fingers linked with hers as they'd strolled after dinner, and their oh-so-magical dance that she relived every night as she fell asleep. Even the mere memory sent a tingling glow from her toes to her scalp. Her eyelids dropped and her head sank forward.

A blast of rap music from a passing car startled her awake, wrenching her head up. Blinking to clear her blurry sight, she looked into the rear-vision mirror, into piercing green eyes. One quick glance from him was all it took to have her feeling vulnerable, as if all her secrets were open for him to read.

How could one look make her tremble? Had there been time to shutter her thoughts? Maybe house-sitting with him living nearby and popping in any time wasn't such a good idea. Scrap that, no *maybe* about it. She could only hope his work, family and friends kept him occupied, and that she had the strength to politely keep him at arm's length.

The house lights were on when he stopped in her driveway; he placed a finger on his lips, nodding towards a sleeping Mel. He left the engine running as he alighted, pushed his door almost shut and opened Cassie's as she reached for the handle. She had no choice but to accept his proffered hand, and didn't resist when he edged her towards the rear of the vehicle, closing her door.

Her unbuttoned coat fell open as he leaned in, placing his hand on the roof of his ute. Even without contact, the heat from his body seared her skin through their clothing. She tried to draw in air, tried to swallow. Tried to remember Mel was nearby.

'Thank you for agreeing to house-sit. It'll be one less worry, and she can relax and enjoy her stay in Melbourne.'

He spoke quietly, his breath tickling her earlobe and his lips brushing her hair. Her heart pounded and her lips tingled. A slight turn of her head would put them within kissing range. Exactly what her illogical side wished for while sensible reasoning feared the consequences.

'It's…not…a problem.' She didn't seem able to talk and think rationally at the same time, forced herself to focus. 'I'd better go in so you can take her home.'

'Mmm. You're right.' He inhaled through his nostrils, but made no attempt to move away. 'Cassie…' Deep and rich, resonating through her.

A motorbike roared past and his head jerked up. Passion and rational thought warred in his dark green eyes, thrilling her even as it triggered alarm bells. She squeezed her eyes shut and curled her fingers. Getting involved would surely end in pain.

So why did she feel cold and alone when he stepped away, craning his neck to check on his aunt. Cassie wrapped her coat tight, skirting past him to the driver's window, from where she could see Mel stirring.

When she opened her eyes and smiled, Cassie went round to say goodnight, and thank her for the evening. Mel let the window down so she could hear.

'You enjoy your time with Janette and the baby when he or she arrives. And don't worry about Sam. I'll walk him every day and take care of your home as if it were mine.'

'I'm sure you will.' Mel kissed her cheek. 'Take care of Jack too. Like all men, he thinks he's immune to human frailties.'

His attitude implied that she was correct as he leant casually on the bonnet waiting. The fluttering in her abdomen, and the ache to have him wrap his arms around her and kiss her senseless, proved she certainly wasn't.

As if there was the slightest chance he would with Mel watching.

'Goodnight, Jack. Thank you for bringing me home. I'll see you on Friday.'

'Goodnight, Cassie. Sweet dreams.'

She kept her back straight as she walked away from him, the warm prickling on the back of her neck proof he watched every step. Fighting the temptation to look towards him before closing the door, she pushed it shut, listening until the engine noise died away.

Cleansing off her make-up, she weighed up the pros and cons of her acceptance. And resolved to cope with the way he affected her because it was never going to be a happy ever after. Their worlds were too different. They were too different.

She slipped into bed, fully aware that, no matter how hard she tried to think of something—anything—else, her sweet dreams would be of him.

Jack watched until the door closed behind her, wondering if she'd dream of him. And who had been peeking through the curtains.

Her light fragrance hung in the air, teasing him. The chilly air had cooled his skin; the fire in his gut still blazed. The aroused male wanted to hear her say she was free, there was no one in her life. The flawed man whose decisions were even now sometimes governed by the consequences of that snowfield trip had an aching feeling it might be better for both of them if she wasn't.

* * *

On Friday Jack pulled into the driveway of Mel's house well in advance of Cassie's four o'clock estimated time of arrival. He unhitched Sam from his harness and let him out, allowing him to race around, glad to be home. Jack followed, strolling through the vegetable garden to the peach tree by the back fence.

Since he'd been old enough to hold a child's trowel, he'd earned blisters digging every patch in this yard. Many of the full-grown productive fruit trees had been planted with his help, and the adults had let the eager young gardener believe they'd survived due to his attentive watering.

No childhood hours could have been better than the ones spent in that way, or assisting Bob in the shed workshop and Mel in the kitchen. What was disguised as fun for his generation had been a solid grounding in self-reliance.

Hunkering down, he scooped up a handful of dirt and let it run through his fingers. He breathed in the pungent aroma and felt his muscles clench. Life went on, evolved and changed. Pain was the price of accepting you couldn't fight fate.

Sometime in the future, nearer than he could bear to contemplate, there'd be a heated swimming pool surrounded by fake lawn in place of the garden. Bob's home-built shed would be demolished in favour of a fashionable man cave, complete with television, bar and pool table.

Though more suited to modern life, none of it could create better memories than those he, his siblings and cousins treasured and often reminisced about. Stealthily harvested fruit, fresh from its source, always tasted better than any served at a table. He plucked a Pink Lady apple from its tree and savoured the tart, ripe taste as he toed his boot into the ground underneath.

Sam's bark alerted him to Cassie's arrival and his melancholy mood evaporated in an instant. Tossing his core onto the compost heap, he strode over to greet her, beaten by the dog, who jumped up as she alighted from the car. He couldn't blame him, felt the urge to get as close as possible too.

'Down, Sam.' Even with its slight edginess, her tone was more encouraging than commanding. Sam sat. Jack wasn't so sure he'd have been so prompt to obey.

'Hi, Jack.' Addressing *him*, her voice was more guarded, indicating she'd decided on a strict courtesy line. His head might agree it was best; every other part of him craved contact, close and physical. Like in his erotic dreams last night.

'Hi, Cassie. Need a hand with your luggage?' He kept the same tone, went to the rear of her car and lifted the boot.

'Thank you. If you take the suitcase and computer satchel, I'll bring my overnight bag and groceries.'

He lifted her luggage without effort, frustration grinding in his gut. If they got any more civil and mundane, he'd be standing to attention.

'Cassie?'

She froze, body bent as she reached for the remaining items. He saw the movement of her shoulders, swore he heard the deep slow intake of air before she reversed into an upright position. Took an age to face him, brown eyes wary.

'Forget it. Let's go inside.' He wasn't sure which displeased him more, her original wariness, her relief at his statement to ignore his tacit plea, or his inconstancy in how he wanted her to act towards him.

Cassie accepted Jack's offer to take her two cases up to the bedroom she'd occupied last week, thankful for the chance to regroup her defences. Telling herself to stay strong and keep her distance had little influence against Jack's smile—heart-stopping yet pulse-stirring—his eyes—irresistible rain-glistened green magnets—and his crackling laugh—an Outback-adventure-transporting melody.

He'd only have to make an entrance at any venue to

have women sending him subtle invitations or blatantly flirting with him. Whatever he said or his glances implied, she was way beneath his social status, and probably just a playful diversion.

She filled the kettle, switched it on and began to unpack the food she'd bought on the way then frowned. Jack hadn't mentioned tonight's meal. Did he intend to have it here, and was she supposed to cook?

If he expected home-baked dessert, he'd be disappointed. Though, as she gaped at the array of appliances on the walk-in larder shelf, she realised staying here gave her a great opportunity to hone her basic skills. The devil in her claimed if he intended to flirt with her he ought to be prepared to act as her guinea pig. Common sense countered she'd be playing with fire and could end up scorched beyond healing.

Why couldn't her head and emotions agree on a common-sense attitude whenever she was with him? Or thought about him. Or dreamt of him.

The hum of the open refrigerator and the bubbling kettle drew Jack to the kitchen door and the tantalising view of Cassie from behind. A few paces forward and her delicate peach scent would stir up more than a hunger for food.

Her thigh-length brown and gold top tightened over her hips as she bent to place something on the bottom shelf. His mouth dried and his chest tightened as his brain flashed back to his first sighting of her under a table. The thud of his heartbeat outraced the tapping of his fingers on his leg.

He had to leave. Now. To prevent him from doing something profoundly stupid, like hauling her into his arms and proving her lips were as sweet and delectable as he fantasised. One kiss would never be enough. Kissing, however deep and numerous, might not be enough.

As silent as he thought he was, she raised her head and paused. Incapable of even breathing, he stood immobile as she straightened up and pivoted. Flanked by the cold interior and the open door, she stood and met his gaze. Whatever she saw in his eyes caused hers to grow bigger, darker. The steady rise and fall of her breasts proved her agitation.

The click as the water reached boiling point seemed too loud, the temperature in the room too high. The distance separating them too great.

'I should go.' The commonplace, sensible words scoured his throat as he forced them out. They weren't the ones jostling in his head. His feet felt leaden, reluctant to walk away from her. His fingers itched to caress her skin.

She gave the slightest of nods and a forced smile. Knowing his attraction was reciprocated made it harder to leave.

'I'll need the keys and security code.' The unique raspy edge in her tone was delightful. He ached to hear it thick with passion.

'Yeah, the box is by the back door.' He led the way, digging into his pocket for the spare set of keys he'd collected from the drawer in the lounge. She brought a notebook and pen from her handbag, and hid the numbers he gave her in a reminder notice about a friend's upcoming birthday.

'Just in case I have a memory lapse.'

She brushed her hand over her hair as she turned to go back to the kitchen, and he recalled that same unconscious action on Tuesday when he'd upset her. Remorse slammed into his gut. He was a self-centred idiot, acting like a coward prepared to run. She had been kind and gentle with Mel and deserved more consideration.

Admit it, you fool. You want to stay.

Hoping he appeared more casual than he felt, he tried for a conciliatory tone. 'Fancy home-delivered pizza for dinner?'

She swung round, features composed, eyes a mixture of caution and hope. 'You're...'

'…Not sure what's happening between us. But running won't change it.'

Since the day the loss of his temper had resulted in tragedy, he'd kept control in any situation, faced the problem and tried for a solution, or at least compromise. His emotions were strictly compartmentalised between family and friends, and others. They were never involved during business transactions and restrained when he dated.

With Cassie, the walls were hazy and he swung from mentally needing to solidify them and physically wanting to breach them. Moments ago, he'd been prepared to walk out, now staying and talking, even for a short while, was his optimum choice.

Keeping eye contact, he walked towards her, stopping within touching distance, his arms loose at his sides.

'I'd like to stay for a while.' His breath caught in his throat and his fingers curled into his palms as he waited for her reply.

She studied him with an intensity that kickstarted heatwaves in his stomach. Talking slid a long way down on his list of activities he'd like to share with her.

'Australian topping with a side of garlic bread. You can choose dessert.' A sudden, mind-boggling smile, a half spin and she'd gone. A surge of tangible pleasure, a huff of exhaled air and he followed, catching up with her as she set two mugs on the kitchen bench.

It was her radiant smile that had crashed his caution and drove him into her personal space, less than his arm's length behind her. A heartbeat away. The set of her shoulders showed she was aware of his close proximity.

'Cassie?' With his fingertip, he traced a circle on her neck, over the pulse below her ear, and saw the resulting tremor rack her body. Desire swept away all reservations. With a gentle hold, he turned her to face him, and found himself even closer.

Near enough to feel the warmth of her body, see the golden sparkle in her eyes and smell the essence that was pure Cassie. His lips were a breath away from hers.

'Conversation won't answer the questions keeping me awake at night.' He slid his hand around her neck. 'Like... how will it feel to have you crushed against me?' He tilted her chin up with his thumb. 'And are your lips as delectable and sweet as I imagine?'

He lowered his head and covered her mouth with his in a tender exploratory kiss. Her body stilled then melted into his, causing an instant physical reaction. His heart blipped, then soared when she didn't pull away. His fingers caressed and firmed as his free arm encircled her waist, binding her to him. His chest expanded and fire flared in his stomach, rapidly spreading to every extremity.

Cassie's arms snaked up and around his neck, her fingers tangled into his hair and he trembled. There was no awareness of time. It was an instant or a lifetime until necessity for air forced his lips from hers barely long enough to gasp and let a possessive male growl escape before settling again. He heard her contented sigh mingle with his low rumble.

The tip of his tongue traced an appeal for entry along her lip line, slipping inside as her lips parted. She tasted even sweeter than he'd imagined, with a hint of something spicy. He stroked and teased the soft flesh, tangled with her tongue and fought the craving for more intimate contact, fought the urge to lift her and...

Flump. A deep doggy sigh shattered the enchantment. Cassie wrenched free, slamming onto the work bench and sending him stumbling away, almost falling over Sam, lying close by.

What the heck? He recovered, glaring at the dog before swinging back to Cassie. His demand for an explanation dried in his throat at the sight of her bright red face. The remorse in her eyes hit him square in the gut, searing him with guilt as she clasped her hands over her mouth and rocked forward and back.

He took a step forward, hands held out in appeal.

'Cassie, what's wrong? Tell me what I did.'

'It's wrong. We can't…we mustn't.' Her hesitant words were muttered against her palms as she dropped her head.

'It felt more than right to me.' Frustration governed his gruff statement; she'd been as willing as him until Sam interrupted them. Her head came up and he locked eyes with her, challenging her to refute his claim. She glared back.

'It's Mel's house. She employs me. Trusts me.'

His spontaneous short bark of laughter startled her. Before she had a chance to recover, he moved in and caught her chin, tilting her head up.

'*Here* is wrong?' Hoarse, as if being forced from his throat. He trailed his knuckles down the side of her face, his lips curling in satisfaction when she quivered.

'Not *me*? Not the *kiss*?'

She blinked under his scrutiny, her brown eyes moist and wary. As if lost for words, she shook her head and he instantly gathered her into a one-armed embrace. His free hand caressed her hair, and her hand landed on his denim shirt over his pounding heart.

She wasn't rejecting him. It was the location. He brushed his lips on her forehead.

'I'd suggest we forgive ourselves that transgression but that would be admitting we're sorry. I'm not. Are you, Cassie?'

'No.' An instant, whispered yet distinct answer. Satisfied that she didn't blame him, he eased away. They both needed recovery time.

'How about you find the cake Mel told me she left in the larder? I'll make coffee. And we'll talk in the lounge.'

CHAPTER ELEVEN

CASSIE CARRIED THE plate of sliced carrot cake, and Jack followed with the steaming mugs. He asked her to hold them, enabling him to move the low table within easy reach of where she liked to sit. Instead of taking Bob's chair, he settled in the centre of the settee, bending his leg on the upholstery, and hooking the other over his ankle.

Her brow furrowed as she swung her head from his usual spot to where he was now, holding out his hand for his coffee. He grinned and quirked an eyebrow, making her smile as she relinquished the mug.

Her pulse blipped at the accidental brush of their fingers. Still keyed up from his kiss, she tried to hide her reaction, selected a piece of cake, sat and wriggled into the end corner of the settee. He faced her, his shoulder pressed against the back, seeming content to just watch her. Didn't drink.

'I meant every word, Cassie. I'm not sorry I kissed you, and I want to again. Even more now I know how… Incredible doesn't come close to describing how good.'

She felt the same; her body still hummed from the rapture of being moulded to his. Her pulse was almost normal yet she knew one special look or even the slightest curl of his full lips would send it rocketing. Every breath she took was imbued with his essence and sandalwood aroma.

'It's not about want.'

She saw his fingers tighten on his mug at her words, saw it shake as he balanced it on his knee. Regretted the loss of tenderness in his eyes.

'There's a lot of places outside Mel's home and you won't be working twenty-four-seven.'

She straightened her spine at his blunt statement. 'No, and…'

'Is there anyone who might have a grievance because I kissed you?'

If it hadn't been for the slight judder in his normally smooth voice, she'd have thought he'd reverted to his suspicions of her the day they'd met. He was as shaken as she was, merely better at concealing it.

'No, there's no one.'

'So we're both free, and we like each other. We can take it easy and see what happens.'

'We can be friends?'

His eyes widened, his eyebrows shot up and he huffed. 'You kiss your *friends* like that, Cassie Clarkson?'

'No! I meant…' She surged forward in distress, shaking her head, and spilling her drink. 'How could you think I'd…?'

Sam was on his feet in an instant, trotting over to her, nudging her hand. Jack scooted along at the same time, dumping his full mug on the table as he went. He took hers from her trembling fingers and placed it alongside. His face contorted with guilt as he cradled hers with his hands.

'I was joking, Cassie. Stupidly trying to cover how mind-blowing it was for me. An immature male reaction to you pulling away first. Forgive me?'

The genuine remorse in his eyes tugged at Cassie's heart. He'd questioned her credentials, and tried gentle pressure when they'd first met; he'd never been cruel. And the oh-so-light feel of his work-roughened hands was turning shaking from dismay into quivers of delight.

There was no way she could voice her certainty of the chasm, cultural and familial, between them. From the day he'd been born, he'd never been alone unless he'd wished it, always had similar age relatives to bounce off and confide in. He'd never had to live within the bounds of a limited budget. And never would.

'I didn't handle it well. It was... I... I've never been kissed like that before.'

Sam nudged again and Jack released her with reluctance, allowing her to stroke the dog.

'I'm okay, Sam.' She ruffled his ears. 'He's very perceptive. It must be comforting to know he's here when Mel's alone.'

'He is, more than most people, including me. Val says my tendency to make jokes about anything emotional is an attempt to hide my insecurities. She knows me better than anyone so she might be right.'

Cassie was stunned at his revelation. She couldn't imagine him sharing this personal information with many people, certainly not a comparative stranger. She felt shy and yet elated.

'I'll try to remember that in future.'

'And I'll try to curb my childish outbursts.'

His lips curled into a stunning smile that rebooted her senses into overdrive. The realisation they were forging a new understanding which needed slow and steady pacing warred with an inexplicable longing for fast and furious.

To hide the blush rising on her cheeks, she bent her head to check her watch. 'Sam must be wondering when his walk's coming.'

'As soon as we settle boundaries.'

Looking up, she encountered glittering eyes and familiar determined features, though without the stern resolve from the past. He wrapped his hands around hers, creating a bond that twined its way to her core.

'While we're here, we'll keep everything light and friendly. Anywhere out in the big wide world, we'll let life unfold and see where it takes us. Agreed?'

They'd be working miles apart. They both had friends

and social lives, and he'd have family commitments. Their time in that big wide world would be limited so it was reasonably safe to comply. But then reason didn't come into how being near him shook her mantra: *Stay strong. Keep distance.*

'Agreed.'

He raised her hands and kissed her knuckles.

'Coffee's cold. Do you want to walk Sam now and order pizza on the way so it's delivered soon after we're home?'

The air cooled as soon as the sun began to set, even on the warmer days they'd been having lately. Clad in thick zippered parkas, they let Sam lead the way, Jack's fingers linking with Cassie's the moment they stepped off the back veranda. A guy had to ensure a lady didn't slip on the damp path, didn't he? And it gave him the added pleasure of her distinctive perfume with every breath.

'Did you have pets as a child?'

Did you learn a musical instrument? Did you like school?

He'd have to limit his questions to general topics at first. And was he prepared to answer any questions she had with the same honesty he expected from her?

'Goldfish for years, and a succession of cats and dogs, always from Animal Welfare. Mum chose older ones who had little chance of being adopted otherwise, and they returned her affection unconditionally.'

She smiled as if recalling a treasured memory. 'The cats and smaller dogs would curl up on her lap as she watched television.'

'Did you have a preference?'

'I loved playing with the dogs, teaching them tricks and trying, not very successfully, to train them. I admired all our cats, who tended to be self-reliant, solitary and often standoffish. And I learned that trust takes time and patience to build.' She laughed teasingly. 'I can't imagine you with cats, more a romp with the pedigree dog type.'

She'd painted a picture of mutts and strays, boisterous fun and limited or no formal training. The complete opposite of the Randell domestic animals. And, without realising, she'd given him an insight into her view of her place in the world when she'd spoken of the cats.

'We always had pedigree dogs, two at all times. The one cat in my lifetime was a present Val bought herself for her fifteenth birthday, still her favourite pet. The dogs were professionally trained but we boys did our best to un-teach them and get them to join in our rough and tumble games.'

'And now?'

'I won't own a dog and leave it alone all day. My cousin had Sam when Mel was in hospital, and he's well behaved so I've taken him with me the last two days.'

He flicked a glance at her, saw her lips part and guessed what was coming. He got in first.

'And no, I'm too old for goldfish and have no interest in an aquarium.'

'Mind-reader.' Their mingled laughter caused a warm glow in his stomach. It sounded natural, nice, something he could get used to. Something he'd miss when she was no longer around.

'Val's threatening to give me a cat for my birthday, says I need the company and something living to take care of. I'm terrified she actually means it.'

'It might do you good to have a flatmate you can't dominate.'

'That's my worry. Can you hold Sam while I make the call?' The alternative was to let go of her hand. Not an option.

Cassie complied, urging the dog to her side. Twilight walking hand in hand with Jack was comforting. She was convinced it could be habit-forming and probably addictive.

Pizza ordered, they walked to the next corner and turned back, Sam remaining under her control.

'When do you intend to start Mel's listing?' Jack asked.

'Tomorrow morning. I have charts in my computer, and I'll do one room at a time.'

She sensed the turn of his head and felt his penetrating gaze. He halted and swung to face her, pivoting her body with his hold. The overhead streetlight reflected in his green eyes reminded her of the lush foliage of a Queensland rainforest. Her body responded in the same way it had trudging up a hill on that hot, steamy day.

'It's the weekend. No days off between contracts?'

'That's what I'm here for. I'll fit in odd hours or days off as I go.'

She wasn't surprised by her heart racing and the fluttering in her stomach, or by the tingles leaping from cell to cell. But how was it possible to feel breathless when her lungs were working overtime pumping air in and out? Especially when his cool fingers caressed her cold cheek and ignited heat.

How was it possible for his eyes to darken any further or to intensify beyond soul-searching? Seconds, minutes—who knew how long the spell lasted?

A raking shudder, a harsh huff of air, and it was broken. He'd wanted to kiss her, and her logical brain silently thanked him for resisting. Her heart regretted his self-control.

'Make sure you do.' Grating, as if from a dry throat, the way hers felt. 'Keep a lookout for the Batman car I lost twenty years ago.'

His hand dropped to his side and they resumed their walk.

'I'm committed for the weekend so if there's anything that needs to be moved or lifted, let it wait. Text me, and I'll get there when I can.'

She had mixed feelings about not seeing him for days. Heck, she had mixed feelings about every aspect of their relationship.

She certainly didn't expect him to be beholden to her because of a kiss. A kiss like no other. A kiss she'd remember for ever.

Cassie was torn when Jack sat in the armchair instead of alongside her. It was more aligned to the television, it did mean they could set the pizza at the end of the table, and it lessened the temptation to shift closer. It also meant he was always either in her peripheral vision or leaning in front of her for food.

They ate all bar two slices of the pizza while watching the news, followed by hot drinks, cheesecake and a multi-times rerun of an American sitcom.

'I'll bet I'll still be laughing at the same gags when I'm old and too deaf to hear the words,' Jack said as the credits rolled up. 'Are you tired or ready for another show?'

She scrolled through the selection.

'Renovations, repeats or reality shows. Unless...there's a sci-fi action film starting in six minutes. Enough time to clear the table, and brew another coffee if you want.'

'What, no popcorn?' His exaggerated aggrieved tone made her laugh, and suddenly it was almost like the evenings at home with Brad and Phil. Almost, because they were like brothers to her, and she'd never ever be able to think of Jack that way.

After the movie finished, they let Sam out for a run before bed. Jack took her hand, walked across the veranda and down a step before twisting to face her.

'It's cold and dark so we'll count this as neutral territory.'

He brushed his lips over hers in a kiss as soft and gentle as the other had been passionate. A swarm of butterflies fluttered in her stomach, generating feather-light sensations from head to toes. Their only physical contact was their lips and linked hands, yet his heat enveloped her, cocooning her from the chilly air.

She swayed forward. He lifted his head. And Sam barked.

Jack's forced smile told her he didn't want to go, the gleam in his eyes said he believed she was beautiful, and his hard kiss on her knuckles confirmed he'd return.

'Sam, inside.'

Keeping his eyes on Cassie's face, he stooped to pat the dog trotting past him.

'Go lock up then I can leave. Sweet dreams, Cassie.'

'Goodnight, Jack.' She turned to smile at him as she closed the door.

A little later, she smiled again as she switched off her bedside lamp and burrowed under the quilt. How could she not have sweet dreams when during her waking hours, he invaded her thoughts with images of slow dancing, moonlight strolls and campfires under the stars?

Cassie wasn't sure what woke her in the night; it might have been a dog barking or a car. There was enough light from the streetlights for her to see the dim shapes of the furniture in the room. She rolled over and the quilt slipped, exposing her shoulders to the chilly air that snapped her to full alert.

She pulled it back but knew there was no point in trying to force sleep. Thinking about the morning ahead might have worked if a vision of Jack hadn't driven every other thought from her mind. Jack, his expression resolute, walking across the foyer towards her after suggesting they order pizza. His eyes had held hers spellbound as he'd narrowed the space between them.

Trying to steady her breathing had meant inhaling sandalwood and Jack's essence, a mixture that scrambled her logic and jellied her insides. She'd ached for him to touch

her, then he'd stunned her with his admission of wanting
to stay, his eyes soft and pleading.

A surge of pleasure had whooshed through her, making her grin like a child on Christmas morning. Words had
shot from her mouth, bypassing her brain and surprising
them both. She'd spun on her heel and fled to the kitchen.

She'd been reaching for a mug when she'd felt his heat
behind her. Every cell in her body had stilled then quivered
at his feather-light caress on her neck. Butterfly tremors
had stirred her stomach and she'd had no resistance as he'd
eased her round, drawn her into his arms and...

He kissed her.

There'd been nothing and no one else in her world. She'd
been conscious of only his touch on her skin, the smoul-
dering fire in his eyes and his firm lips settling over hers.

Unexpectedly soft and cautious, his kiss had provoked
liquid warmth low in her belly, exhilarating prickles that
raced across her skin and an overwhelming desire to nestle
tight into his body, eliminating even the air between them.

Time had stood still. His lips had lifted and she'd sighed,
heard and felt his grunt of pleasure rumble up his chest,
and sighed again when they resettled on hers.

His arms had tightened, moulding her to his frame. She'd
woven her fingers into his hair, rejoiced at his trembling.
Her lips parted, allowing him entry, and the outside world
had evaporated in a burst of sensations she could never
have imagined.

Kissing had never been this sensual, so astonishingly
thought-draining, so breathtakingly thrilling. He'd tasted
of strong coffee with tart apple, and a craving for more of
both enveloped her. More tang, more flavour. More Jack.
She was weightless, soaring...

Flump.

Sam. Mel. Mel's house...

Remorse had shaken her, as hot and soul-searing as

Jack's kisses. How had she so easily forgotten where she was, who she was?

Pushing him away, slamming her spine on the work bench as she'd stepped back, and then dithering over an explanation hadn't helped. Only when his irritated retort had sparked a clear response from her had he understood she wasn't upset because he'd kissed her. And he'd made it quite clear he'd like to repeat the incredible experience, away from Mel's home.

In the clear light of day, she'd argue the wisdom of complying. Alone in the blanket of night, she snuggled deeper, closed her eyes and let herself drift back into sweet dreams of that moment to come.

CHAPTER TWELVE

HER RESERVATIONS KICKED back in when her alarm woke her at seven o'clock. Being friends with Jack would be nigh on impossible given the magnetism that drew them to each other whenever they met. That original spark threatened to flare into bushfire heat with each encounter.

Now that they'd kissed, *twice*, once hot and heady, and later so tender and sweet, she feared her heart was already defenceless.

Standing under the hot shower, she resolved to be stronger, certain she could be when he wasn't around, not so sure if he smiled at her, touched her or gave that special crackling laugh.

A folding card table from the family room served as a desk upstairs for the laptop, printouts and her mobile. After the third call on Mel's landline, she took the cordless phone wherever she went. There had also been two women who'd opened the back door and called out.

On Monday evening Val popped in, chatted over coffee about her weekend in Melbourne and promised to visit regularly. Cassie liked her, hoped she would. During her last stay, she'd heard Mel receive numerous calls and deduced she had a wide circle of friends as well as her large family. She'd met a few while Mel had been there but Cassie hadn't realised how many of them phoned or visited on a regular basis.

To her disappointment, just two calls had been from Jack, the first late on Saturday night as she'd prepared for bed. He'd sounded tired, asked about her day and said his had been gruelling but productive. Without elaborating, he'd wished her sweet dreams.

On Sunday afternoon, she'd heard childish squeals, voices and a chainsaw in the background, almost drowning out his voice. Again, he'd kept it short, almost business-like, until the end when one of those children had demanded Uncle Jack's attention. His 'Gotta go' had dampened her already low mood further. His whispered 'Miss you, Cassie' had sent her heart soaring. So much for keeping distance, even when they were.

Whenever she took a break, she wandered round the house studying the photographs that adorned every room. Being able to pick out Jack as a toddler gave her a warm glow of satisfaction, and from that she followed his life through school and into maturity.

She found one she presumed was taken at a high school formal. He had his arm around a very attractive blue-eyed brunette who wore her red figure-hugging ballgown with the confidence and grace of a model. The way they posed, bodies close and relaxed, their smiles natural, proved they were dating.

The girl's image stayed with her all day. Where was *she* now? Had the teenage romance failed the test of moving into the working world? Who had ended the relationship?

Jack hadn't rung by the time she fell asleep. She had no right to expect a daily call, text or visit. She'd had no reason to call or text him.

So he'd kissed her, turning her muscles into jelly. So he'd said he wanted to kiss her again, and then given her an almost-not-there brush of his lips. *To be fair, it was still the second most thrilling kiss of her life.* So he'd told her he wanted to get to know her, and had said little more than hello and goodbye over the phone in three days.

Hadn't she been telling herself not to let his charm override her caution since the moment they'd met?

* * *

Her ringtone woke her from a deep sleep. She blinked, noted faint light around the curtains and groped for her phone. Didn't check the caller ID as she held it to her ear, and began to drift back to sleep.

'Cassie?'

'Jack?' Caution evaporated with one word. Every sense sprang to alert as she struggled up onto one elbow. 'What's wrong? What time is it?'

'Early, darling. It was too late to call last night. The forecast is for sunshine and I'm free until eleven.' His voice was animated and alive, in contrast to their last two short conversations.

'Do you and Sam want to come for breakfast and a walk on the beach? There's a café ten minutes' walk from here, and they'll be opening soon.'

She sank back and stared at the ceiling. He'd barely spoken to her since that last spine-tingling brush of lips, and now he expected her to drop everything she had planned and race to his side.

'Cassie? You've worked for eight days straight—time for a break. I'll come and pick you up.'

'No. I'll drive.' How could she refuse? 'And, before you say anything, I've had a GPS for years, and now I've got a car harness for Sam. All I need is where you live.'

'Smart as well as beautiful.' His laughter crackled along the line.

As she stepped into the shower a delicious flood of adrenaline swamped her. Jack had called her 'darling'.

Jack leant on the railing of his bedroom balcony, watching the waves through the gap between the houses across the road. He knew he was grinning, and didn't want to stop. Between meetings regarding his shopping centre enterprise, scheduled work at his rental properties and a commitment to attend his nephew's birthday, he'd hardly had time to eat or sleep since Friday night.

Through it all, Cassie and those two kisses had hovered at the back of his mind, surging into prominence whenever he took a break, or settled in bed at night. How come there were times he could be so logical and reinforce all the reasons they shouldn't get involved, and yet when she was near, or he recalled the way her eyes shone or her sweet smile, logic and reason dissipated? Leaving only yearning and the anticipation of something new and extraordinary.

His determination to never get too involved with another woman was based on logic and his acute awareness of his flaws and weaknesses. He knew little about Cassie's personal life and friends, and almost nothing of her family background.

He did know he'd missed her. She'd agreed to come for breakfast with him. He'd have a chance to claim a third kiss, maybe more.

Cassie didn't need the disembodied voice of the satnav to tell her they were nearing Jack's home. Sam strained towards the rear right window, head up, body quivering with excitement. *Her* body reacted in the same way at the sight of the familiar figure waiting by the brick and iron fence of a modern two-storey glass and tan house with twin balconies on the top floor.

As she slowed down, he walked to the kerb, waiting until she'd stopped before opening the passenger door. His smile was warm and inviting, the dark shadows under his eyes indicating a lack of sleep. He lifted her bag from the seat, slid in and held it on his lap.

'Hi, Cassie.' Leaning across the central column, he kissed her lips. A brief touch that blew away her vexation for his lack of communication since Friday, replacing it with heartfelt longing. So not the cool, calm mindset she'd sworn to have.

'Drive straight into the garage.' He glanced between the seats. 'Hi, Sam, ready for a walk?' The answering *woof* echoed in the enclosed space.

Their entrance automatically activated overhead lights in the spacious garage running the length of the house. Cassie parked behind Jack's ute and stepped out, staring in amazement. This was the cleanest, tidiest workshop area she'd ever seen, and she'd been in quite a few.

A wide bench cupboard stretched about two-thirds of the way along the right-hand wall, ending at the rear, where there was a matching roller door to the back garden. On top of the bench—absolutely clear except for a chainsaw in pieces—were a mixture of cupboards and shelves for the length of his ute. Shadow boards displaying tools and equipment covered the remaining wall space.

Everything was packed neatly away, nothing out of place, no oil spills on the floor. The one incongruity was the large framed painting hanging on the wall next to the door leading into the house. It depicted a mountain in winter, reminiscent of holiday brochure photos for the ski season in the Snowy Mountains. Its snow-covered peaks led the eyes down to increasing expanses of trees on the lower slopes.

Why had he deliberately placed it so it was in his direct eyeline whenever he came home?

'Cassie?'

She turned to find Jack, with an amused expression, and Sam, head tilted and tail wagging, waiting for her by the boot of her car.

'Sam and I are hungry.'

So was she, and not just for food. She drank in the sheer masculinity of him, from his colourful runners to his natural mussed light brown hair. In his tan chinos, brown polo neck sweater and zip-up green jacket he epitomised an outdoor man. The idea of him spending his life wearing a suit and sitting in front of a computer in an air-conditioned office was absurd.

And so was the soft bright red patterned zip-up bag hanging on his shoulder. She burst out laughing, startling man and dog, who exchanged puzzled looks. Lifting it off, she slipped it over her head then gave him a once-over.

'Much better for your image. Let's go.'

'Ladies first.'

He glanced back at the painting as she passed him, deepening her intrigue. Once he'd closed the roller door, he pocketed his keys and took her hand, enclosing it in his. The air was cooler than she'd expected, justifying her choice of jeans and roll-neck jumper beneath her wool-blend jacket. Winter socks and sneakers kept her feet warm. She rarely wore gloves or anything on her head.

'I like the garden. Your work?' In truth, she loved the setting of pebble stones and three large rocks, interspersed with ground cover and plants of varying heights, different shades of green and some with bright coloured leaves.

'My plan, plus a barbecue for family and friends who helped. I'll show you the back yard later.'

'It's an impressive home. Not very old, from the style.' She daren't imagine the size of the mortgage, if he even had one. Family connections might have helped out there.

'It was a lucky break for me as I knew the couple who were building. He was offered a promotion entailing a five-year stint in the States a few days after the foundation had been poured. I took over their contract, negotiated a few changes, and moved in mid-December two years ago.'

Jack was well aware of how lucky he'd been. A short time earlier, the couple would have cancelled the contract and sold the empty block. A month later and he'd have already invested his equity in another property. He was also convinced that luck followed those who planned ahead, and were able to take advantage of it.

A gust of wind caught them at the corner leading down to the esplanade. Two women power-walked along the sand, a large black Labrador bounding beside them. Seagulls circled above them, squawking loudly before dipping towards the sea. He turned to Cassie and her radiant smile dried his throat, preventing speech.

'Mum used to call this brisk. Cool morning air with a nip in the breeze. I love it.'

It showed. That breeze stirred strands of her hair, blowing them over her chilled red cheeks. Her eyes sparkled as if this were a big adventure, and her smile gave him the credit for arranging it. His chest swelled as he sucked in cold air, and his heartbeat raced, faster than when he ran. He'd happily accept any acclaim, especially if it furthered their friendship.

'You're not too cold? I ought to have told you to bring gloves and a beanie. Or lent you one of mine.'

'And mess up my hair? You're not wearing one.' She laughed, the sweet sound wrapping around him, enticing him to pull her closer to his side.

'I'm used to it. Uh-huh, not chauvinistic.' He pre-empted her next words. 'I run in the mornings as often as I can. It definitely gets the adrenaline going during the cold months.'

They stopped to cross the road, Sam straining to get to the sand.

'Heel, Sam. Breakfast first.'

The café was a short walk along the esplanade, with outside seating under large umbrellas. Sam settled next to a large ceramic bowl filled with clean water in the corner. Jack dropped the leash on the ground, held the canvas seat with an ocean view for Cassie then sat by her side.

'I'm having the big breakfast and coffee, and I guarantee whatever you fancy will be fresh and tasty,' Jack said, not bothering to check the menu. 'A solid run, a hot meal and I'm ready for the day. Hi, Sue.'

He introduced Cassie to the waitress, who owned and ran the business with her husband. They shared a joke as she wrote down his order plus two grilled meat patties for Sam, though he was aware of Cassie's gaze flicking up and down the menu as if rereading the items would help her select one.

'Too many choices? Pick one and have another next time.' He loved the way her brows arched, as if questioning his mind-reading ability.

Loved? Figure of speech.

She finally placed the menu down with a soft *huff* and smiled at Sue.

'I'll have a ham omelette, please, and an apple and ginger tea. I've never tried that flavour.'

'It's delicious and refreshing. Won't be long.'

Jack arched his back, gave Cassie a rueful grin when she noticed and her expression became thoughtful.

'It's been a hectic three long days. Didn't get home till near eleven last night, too late to call.' Because he'd missed her and her unique voice, and wouldn't have been able to keep it short.

'You look tired. It might have been better if you'd slept in.'

He gave her his best horrified stare. 'And miss breakfast with you two.'

Her laughter was worth any number of hours sleep.

'This week it's back to normal. Can I come to dinner tonight?'

His abrupt question startled Cassie. A picture of old-fashioned domestic bliss flashed into her head; a cosy dinner for two, hot and ready for the man of the house the moment he arrived home from work. Candles and music and…

'*Awk.*' A seagull swooped to the ground right by their table to scoop up a discarded scrap of food. Sam barked and the vision dissolved in a pang of regret. Jack's arrogant smirk didn't help.

'See, I even provide tableside entertainment.'

She tilted her head, and pursed her lips.

'You? Hmm. Okay, give us an encore.'

'Well, um. Ah, saved by the lady bearing drinks.'

Cassie sipped the hot, invigorating tea, enjoying its tart flavour, and trying to recall what they'd been talking about before. Oh, yes. Jack's request. She looked up into appealing green eyes and wondered if anyone ever refused him. Her normally coherent brain certainly couldn't come up with a single reason.

'I'm a basic cook, nothing fancy like you're probably used to.'

His face darkened for a second then cleared, so fast she might have imagined it. The fingers of his hand flattened out on the table, his chest rose and fell and his penetrating eyes held hers captive.

'Is that how you see me, Cassie? Part of the elite who dine rather than eat, are served rather than cook, and expect to have their wineglasses refilled throughout the meal?'

'No!' Her cup clinked as she abruptly set it down. Her stomach churned and her cheeks burned with shame. 'How could you think that? I know your family is well off, and you often have meals with Mel, who has great culinary skills, but you bought hamburgers that morning and...'

'I'm an idiot who just overreacted.' He reached out and lifted her hand, cradling it in his, and stroking her knuckles with his thumb in a slow, mesmerising motion. 'A throwback to teenage years defending my family status from contemporaries who thought I believed I was superior.'

'*I don't.*'

He threw back his head and laughed. She realised her

ambiguity, and pulled her hand away in remorse. Closing her eyes made it worse as her mind conjured up chops and onions grilling over a crackling campfire. Complete with tantalising smells.

'Here we are.'

Her eyes flew open to a view of a fluffy omelette garnished with parsley being lowered in front of her. The stronger aromas making her mouth water were from Jack's meal in Sue's other hand.

Big breakfast? It was *huge*, more than she normally ate in a whole day—bacon, two fried eggs, two sausages, tomato, mushrooms and a hash brown. She was still staring when Sue returned with a rack of toast, a dish of scrolled butter and the two patties on a disposable plate for Sam.

'You're going to eat all that?'

'A working man needs sustenance. This, and a sandwich for lunch, will keep me going until dinner when I'm active.' Jack picked up his cutlery and began to eat. 'Other less physical days, I cut back. Aren't you going to eat? Tastes better hot.'

'So you're working this afternoon.' She began to eat her omelette. It was delicious, lighter and tastier than she'd ever been able to achieve.

'Yeah, and it's this side of town so I can be with you before seven. If I'm still welcome?'

He phrased the remark as a question, putting the burden of veto on her. She didn't answer, ate and thought, weighing up the risks. More contact meant more chance—no, certainty—of closer involvement. He'd already proved how easily he could obliterate any resistance to his touch. If—when—he kissed her again, would she be able to fortify her defences enough to say no, should he try to take it further?

She raised her head and found him watching her with such a hopeful expression her heart flipped and the sudden sharp wrench to her stomach left her breathless.

Dropping her gaze was an instinctive action to hide the answer he'd have no trouble reading. She wouldn't refuse him but appearing too eager would give him the advantage.

Yeah, as if he doesn't already know he has it. You can't keep distance. Try to stay strong.

CHAPTER THIRTEEN

JACK REACHED FOR his coffee mug and drank the strong brew. At the time of suggesting they spend time together, he'd told himself finding out more about her would protect his aunt. Now he knew he'd been deceiving himself.

His resolve to treat Cassie with detached respect in consideration to Mel, and to Cassie herself, was being undermined by his attraction for her, the desire to see her, touch her, and hear her edgy voice which always sent his pulse racing.

Sitting across the table from her was pure pleasure. He'd be happy to stay here all day, and drink in the soft sheen of her dark hair, the delicate curve of her silk-smooth cheeks and her red lips with their tiny quirk.

She'd looked down so quickly he hadn't been able to gauge her response. A controlled man, unlike the easily provoked teenager he'd been, he'd learnt anything worth having was worth waiting for. He finished his meal and was draining his coffee mug when she pushed her plate away and made eye contact. In an unusual occurrence for him, he couldn't read the message in her sombre contemplation.

'I'm pushing too hard, aren't I? It's as if… Hell, I can't explain. Let's eat and walk. I'll abide by whatever decision you make before you go home.'

If he'd told her the truth, she'd think he was crazy. Since he'd kissed her, he'd had a sense of being on restricted time, and he had no idea why or what for. He didn't believe in hunches or premonitions, basing his life on solid facts and experience.

He'd never lacked confidence with women, found it easy

to approach someone he fancied. Cassie was like no one he'd ever met, independent yet vulnerable, prepared to stand up to him yet mindful of her employed position. With her, he wasn't sure of the rules of play but her enchanting smile and simple nod of acceptance satisfied him.

He went inside to pay, leaving Cassie to finish her tea and stir up Sam who, happy and fed, was curled up, dozing. They waited for him on the footpath, Cassie hunkering down to scratch Sam's ears. He was shuddering with delight, his tail sweeping the ground as she talked to him, and Jack knew exactly how he felt.

Two heads turned and two pairs of solemn eyes regarded him for a second then Sam barked a greeting and Cassie's lips curled into an encouraging smile before she spoke.

'Chicken stir-fry with rice? No critiquing allowed.'

'Not even if it's positive?' He made a mental *Yes!* gesture in his head, tempering the urge to say it out loud and punch the air.

'I'll take that in writing.' She laughed and relinquished control of the dog.

He took the leash, relishing the now familiar ripple that flowed through him at her musical sound, and linked their fingers. They crossed the road towards the beach.

Although the sun shone, the breeze had picked up during their meal on the sheltered veranda. Maybe this wasn't such a great idea? Would it be better to go back to his house, and invite her another day when it was warmer?

Cassie noticed a few hardy swimmers keeping a good pace through the water, arms and legs pumping them along. She admired the resilience of the surfers sitting out there on their boards, legs dangling in the surf, waiting for a perfect wave. Not understanding why their muscles didn't cramp from limited motion in this cold weather, she shivered, hugging her jacket tighter.

'Too cold?' Jack let go of her hand and slipped his arm around her, drawing her closer to his side.

She shook her head. He'd invited her for a walk and she'd hold him to it.

'No, I'm fine. Wouldn't be out *there* for anything, though.'

'Wetsuits and adrenaline nullify the cold when you catch a good wave. Sure you don't want to try?'

She picked up on the challenge in his voice.

'Not until summer.' Slipping from his hold, she stepped onto the sand and headed for the sea.

'It's a date.' He came after her, almost knocking her over when she suddenly swung around. He caught her by the waist to steady her, dark green eyes gleaming.

'That's not...'

'No chickening out. And—' he pressed a quick kiss on her lips to stifle her protest '—we can hire or borrow a wetsuit your size.' Arms outstretched, he scanned her body, and wriggled his eyebrows. 'Slender perfection.'

She tapped his chest in mock displeasure. 'Idiot.'

He unclipped Sam's lead, ordering him to stay close before letting him go.

'Isn't he supposed to be kept on a leash?' There were signs clearly stating council regulations.

'Kept *under control*. He won't go more than a few metres from us even if another dog comes near. Unless it threatens you or me, and then a firm "Stay, Sam" will have him sitting, but ready, between us and the danger.'

'He's a credit to whoever trained him.'

'Bob and Mel, with help, and I use the term loosely, from any child who visited. Let's go.'

He retook her hand and they strolled along the shoreline, passing morning joggers and dog walkers, many giving their pets a free romp in the sea. Jack hadn't been kidding;

Sam ran ahead then either splashed in the foam until they reached him or loped back

Jack described the different moves and stances the surfers made on their journey to the shore, and claimed tongue-in-cheek he could have been a champion. She admitted to giving up after not being able to stand up in motion.

'Wait till you try with an expert coach.' His attempt to look humble made her laugh.

'Humility's not your style, Jack Randell.'

He joined in. 'You wouldn't want me to lie, would you?'

This was nice, friendly. Comfortable. She'd be content to stroll all day, talking casually about the world around them or in companionable silence.

They were within sight of the café on the return trip when they stopped to laugh at a black and white terrier challenging the might of the ocean. Focused on his antics, they were oblivious to undulation behind them until the water swirled around their shoes.

Cassie skittled up the sand, looked back, and stilled. She held her breath and clasped a hand to her chest as a lump formed in her throat. This was one of those special moments to be stored away and brought out when her spirits needed a boost.

She turned her head from left to right, noting every sight and sound. The sun's radiance, tempered by banks of clouds being blown across the sky, a cruise ship on the horizon, inciting holiday dreams, and the surfers weaving their way to shore. This backdrop, the people and their pets, were essential images of the whole. And in centre foreground stood Jack, now on firm sand, arms folded, head slightly tilted, regarding her with a quizzical expression.

Closing her eyes, she seared the panorama into her mind for the future. Not enough—the urge for something more tangible gripped her. Her phone was out in an instant and she snapped him before he had the chance to protest or alter that look. Took two more for insurance.

She would now be able to see Jack, wind-blown hair, tanned skin and athletic body, any time, wherever she was, wherever he was. She gasped as reality struck and her arm dropped to her side. Hard bands of steel bound her lungs and an iron fist squeezed her heart. He was everything her dream man should be—except she didn't fit in his world and, with her lack of proven family, never would.

He noticed the change. Brow furrowed, he strode over, catching her by the shoulders. The intensity of his gaze seared and she couldn't control her trembling.

'What is it, Cassie? The cold? We'd better go back.'

'No, I...'

It's you who makes me tremble and stirs emotion I can't control.

Not to be uttered out loud. And she had no chance anyway, as he lowered his head and covered her mouth with his, so gentle at first then deeper as she responded. His arms stroked her back before settling into a firm hold, and hers slid around his waist to complete the embrace.

The sounds around them muted into the background. His sandalwood cologne mingled with her peach fragrance, creating a unique blend with every inhalation. And the rich coffee taste of him invigorated and enthralled her.

Jack had no sense of place or time. He was lost in the ecstasy of having this woman in his arms, her lips returning his kiss with an ardour that threatened to undermine his control. She roused a stronger desire than he'd ever felt in his life.

With supreme effort, he raised his head and eased his body away before he embarrassed them both. How would she react if he voiced his preferred way to warm them both?

Her wistful eyes told him he hadn't been alone in his

fantasy. Prior to his kiss, they'd been clouded with despair, and for some reason he'd felt himself the cause.

He'd watched her gazing seaward, slowly turning her head to take it all in, an enchanting smile on her face. She'd been fine until she'd snapped a photo of him. He'd seen her chest rise, her lips purse and her arm drop slowly to her side, and instantly moved to find out why. She'd quivered at his touch, and he couldn't explain why the motion spread up his fingers and throughout his body.

Kissing her had been an instinctive action and, despite his physical response in a public place, he'd never regret the impulse. He touched her cheek, gently stroked two fingertips on the soft underside of her chin, silky soft, cool to his touch.

'Hold that thought, darling. Hot chocolate and dunking biscuits await us at home.'

One blink, a tiny *huff*, and her face cleared. She looked at Sam, lying patiently nearby, his head on his front paws.

'I'll need Sam's leash.' Hearing Jack say his name, the dog trotted over and sat beside them to be harnessed. Cassie unzipped her shoulder bag and held it out. The brush of their fingers proved the heat of their kiss hadn't waned.

The journey home was quicker, due to the enticement of warmth and hot drinks. They entered through the garage then Jack unlocked the door leading into the house. Cassie was immediately aware of the warmth inside but not so distracted that she didn't notice his quick glance at the painting. She wondered if he was aware of the tension and release of his fingers on hers.

He waved her into a laundry with a bathroom at the far end. The equipment was top brand as expected, the lack of any normal clutter astonishing. No cleaning products in sight, no clothes in a basket or piled on the washing machine. As neat and tidy as his garage. Okay, so he had an excellent cleaning service.

And gets his work ute detailed?

Without a word, she followed him into a hallway wide enough to allow for the wooden staircase with cupboard space beneath. The walls were painted light tan, and all other surfaces varnished to showcase the natural detail.

Jack released Sam who, obviously a regular visitor, shot off towards the back of the house.

'I keep bowls and a bed handy for when he stays over,' Jack explained. 'Turn around and I'll take your jacket to hang up.' Did he deliberately let his fingers glide over her neck, knowing how her body would respond?

He shrugged his off, and hung both in the closet by the front door. His eyes shone with pride as he gestured to the rooms on either side.

'Welcome to my home, Cassie. Lounge on my left and spare room right; open kitchen and dining, plus family room down the hall. My study, two bedrooms and main bathroom upstairs. Would you like to explore while I make the hot chocolate?'

Yes, of course she did, very much. Admitting it was a different matter; it would be like invading his privacy. His lips curved and his eyes twinkled brighter at her hesitancy.

'You want to. Remember I've got two sisters and numerous female cousins. They all love sticky-beaking in other people's houses. Enjoy.' He kissed her cheek and followed Sam.

Cassie took a step the same way, stopped, and swung towards the stairs. She did like seeing the different ways people furnished and decorated their homes, the personal touches that told of their lives. And this exclusively designed house would reveal his true character.

She peeked into the bedrooms, unsure which was his. Both were showroom neat with double beds, one blue themed and the other green. The study contained all the fittings of a city office, not even a paperclip out of place. They were all well-furnished and stylish, a tribute to the decorator. However, it was the bathroom that had the wow factor for her.

The shower was big enough for two, and the deep free-standing bath had a view out of the window, presumably one way only. The marble wall tiles and double basin vanity complemented each other with limited patterning streaks of light grey and red. Everything shone with cleanliness, even the chrome fittings, and there were no toiletries, no toothbrush or holder in sight. She was fascinated by the pristine mirror the length of the vanity.

The niggling doubt that had begun in his workshop grew with each room she visited. It had nothing to do with the furniture and fittings, which were manly and tasteful. The colours were neutral, and wall decorations consisted of a few bold paintings and family photographs in matching frames. A similar, smaller alpine painting to the one in the garage hung, a deliberate distance from the large wall-mounted television, in direct eyeline of anyone walking into the lounge room.

Domestic help had to be the answer. Apart from proving he was minimalist in taste with few adornments, nothing seemed out of place. Even the television remote sat neatly in a holder on the coffee table. She felt an irrational desire to pick up and casually toss down the large bright blue cushions on the extra-long burgundy leather sofa.

This was too organised for a bachelor's home. She'd lived with two men for nearly three years now, dividing cooking and chores, and had other male friends, single and married. For most of them, housework was something to be avoided if possible, or done with minimum exertion when it could not be put off any longer.

Moving to the back of the house, she was impressed with

the open-plan across its breadth. Glass doors led out onto a covered, paved patio and lawn. Garden beds of colourful shrubs and occasional small ornamental trees ran along the three fence lines. An ideal setting for summer barbecues.

She ran her fingers over the smooth top of the round dining table, part of a rich reddish-brown wood grain suite. Beautiful. And yet…for a moment, she was lost in a daydream of a cosy home with comfy furniture and normal scattered family possessions.

Shaking it away, she turned towards the kitchen area. The sight of Jack watching her as he waited by the marbled stone bench top, near two steaming mugs and a plate of biscuits, threw her for a moment. In the silence, as she'd wandered, it had felt as if there could not be a living soul in this immaculate house with no personal stuff lying around.

CHAPTER FOURTEEN

HER BREATH CAUGHT in her throat and tiny flares of heat swamped her body as her eyes feasted on his muscular torso and arms, firmly shaped by his polo neck top. Recalling their first meeting and her full scan of his body, the inevitable blush spread up her face, heating her skin.

'Do you actually live here?' Her hand flew to her mouth to stifle her gasp. What she'd been thinking had slipped out without censorship.

Jack's spontaneous laughter made her feel worse.

'I'm sorry—that was rude and...'

'No, you're right. It is very show-homey, isn't it? It is, however, practical for the life I lead.' He grinned. 'Except for the guys' pizza and sports watching nights.'

'Men only? That's sexist,' she teased, glad he wasn't offended.

'It would be if it wasn't the women who declared we should be segregated. They're welcome to join us any time. So are you.'

She hadn't realised she'd moved forward until he reached out and caught her hand, bringing her closer with little effort. His arms enfolded her, giving her little choice but to lay her hands on his chest. There was no doubting the strength and firmness of his muscles under the material. Or the steely intention in his green eyes and her own willingness to comply.

Her pulse stuttered as he lowered his head. He crushed her against him and she felt his heart pounding. Her own erratic beat throbbed at every pulse point. His mouth settled over hers, and she heard her own sigh of contentment.

His lips caressed and teased, claimed and possessed. Hers complied and tempted, provoked and soothed. And parted at his request. She heard his sharp intake of air, took one of her own and inhaled his unique aroma and the salty smell of the sea.

His tongue tangled with hers, stroked the soft flesh and aroused a longing for unknown pleasures that could be hers if she surrendered. Digging her fingernails into his shoulders, she raised up onto her toes and arched her back. The warning bells ringing in her head were ignored.

Suddenly his lips broke free, his forehead rested on hers and his chest heaved. She couldn't breathe, her knees were buckling, and his strong embrace was the only reason she hadn't sunk to the floor.

'Cassie—' rough as if he'd swallowed sandpaper '—I want you. More than I've ever wanted anyone before.'

He traced trembling fingers down her cheek, and she sucked in a shaky breath. Her touch on his jaw evoked a convulsion of his Adam's apple.

'I swore I wouldn't let kissing you get out of hand this morning. Not when I have to leave in an hour.'

She jerked back, her stomach clenching. He'd driven her to the brink of surrender, and now he wanted to stop? She tried to push him away but he stood solid, arms firm around her, dark green eyes locked with hers.

'Having you near makes me forget everything else. I wanted to spend time with you, meant to keep it friendly. The way you looked at me made it impossible not to kiss you. I swear I didn't mean to lose control.'

His eyes pleaded for her to understand. How could she not when she'd been as uninhibited as him?

'You weren't alone,' she replied, struggling to keep her voice from breaking.

'Oh, darling, I know that.' He pressed a quick kiss on her brow. 'When we make love, I want time to hold and caress you, make every moment pleasurable with no time restraints.'

His hands slid over her hips then stilled. She felt his shoulders lift as he inhaled, felt his warm breath on her skin as they fell.

He *wanted* her. No promises of undying devotion, or happy ever after. Yet not in the quick-romp-under-the-sheets way either. She wanted him, more than she'd ever known it was possible to desire a man. She so wished he'd carried her to his bedroom and taken her now, while she was consumed with heat and longing.

By tonight common sense and logic would have resurfaced, and they'd be meeting in Mel's home. She'd be governed by her rules of propriety. He'd respect her wishes and might have realised staying platonic was best for them both.

With deliberate care, she steadied her breathing and stepped back, hoping her eyes didn't betray her regret. His arms fell to his sides, letting her go, the remorse in his eyes blatant and unrepentant.

'Our drinks are getting cold.' Her rasping voice gave her away but he quirked a smile and reached for the mugs.

'Let's go into the lounge. You bring the biscuits?'

Cassie led the way, pummelling one of those big bold cushions before settling into it. Jack sat an arm's length away and held out her drink.

'Try a dunker, and tell me what you think.'

'Dunker?' She'd thought they were shortbread, now realised they were firmer, less crumbly. Her still-raised pulse blipped as he flashed his playful smile.

'Have to be dunked into a hot drink. Minimum five seconds. It's the rule.'

She did as he said and the biscuit melted in her mouth with a burst of unique flavour. A drink of the hot chocolate straight after had her smiling with delight.

'No way these came in a packet,' she stated. 'Have to be Mel's.'

His eyebrows shot up and he feigned an insulted expression. 'Really?'

'I can tell the diff... Oh.'

Jack loved her confusion, loved the gentle blush that coloured her skin, and fought the urge to reach out to touch and reassure.

'You made them? You cook?'

'Can you imagine any child who spent time with Mel not becoming proficient in the kitchen? Come back tonight and I'll prove it.'

His offer surprised him, as did the warm glow of anticipation in his stomach. Followed by a twinge of apprehension. Going to her would be safer, more prudent. His rules of no involvement were changing. He was changing and, inexplicably, he wasn't sorry.

She looked down at the biscuit and mug she held, her top lip covered the bottom lip then drew back. He dunked, bit, drank and waited.

She finally raised her head. 'Yes. What's your favourite colour?'

What the heck? He watched her lips curve and her eyes sparkle. And understood.

'Don't have one. Yours?'

'Blue or red for clothes, neutral and red for décor, silver for cars.'

'Yours is blue?'

'I got a good deal. Favourite male singer?'

By the time she left, they'd joked, laughed and learnt a lot of random facts about each other. As he watched her drive away, he was acutely aware that it was all surface detail. Deeper feelings and emotions had been avoided.

* * *

Cassie picked at the sleeves of the V-neck jumper she wore, uncertain if it was suitable for…for what? Seduction on a winter's evening? This was dinner at his house, and he'd be bringing her home after.

She stood up and paced, ran her hands down her thighs and huffed out a breath. Sucked in a deeper one at the sound of his ute.

It was dinner at his house. Nothing more, unless she wanted it to be. The sensible side of her brain advised caution. Her body and heart clamoured *yes, yes*. Yes. Regret for things not done could be more powerful than for bad decisions taken.

Common sense flew off with the wind when she met Jack at the corner of the house. She ran into his open arms, and was lifted onto his chest. Tangling her fingers into his hair, she gave herself up to the magic his lips wove as they covered her mouth in a tender kiss.

She pressed closer, melting inside, and exulted in the animal growl rising in his throat. It was no longer *if* but *when* they'd make love. Preferably sooner, as the time limit of their relationship was unknown.

The shudder he gave as he broke the kiss and set her on her feet excited her. She'd been the cause, a delicious fact to remember in the future.

'Temptress. Let's go before I…'

He left the rest of the sentence unsaid and she tingled at the images her imagination created.

'You'd better say hello to Sam before we lock up.'

His eyes darkened and he spoke slower and softer than normal, betraying stress she hadn't expected.

'You're leaving him here?'

'I'll be coming home.'

Please accept my decision without question.

For a moment, she thought he'd argue but he let it go with a curt nod.

Studying him as he drove, she became aware of a vague sense that something didn't gel. He wore the same clothes as this morning, but that wasn't it.

'Problem, Cassie? You look perplexed.' He flicked her a quick glance.

'I'm not sure.'

He was heart-stoppingly cowboy handsome—macho features, hypnotic green eyes and strong jaw. *His jaw?*

'Did you go home before picking me up?'

'No, why?'

That first day at Mel's he'd been stubbled. She wasn't sure about other occasions but he definitely hadn't been any time they'd kissed.

'You've shaved.'

'Glad you noticed. Check the glovebox.'

Would she ever be immune from his special chuckle? She checked, and pulled out a rechargeable shaver.

'I've used it more in the last two weeks than the previous few months. Wanna guess why or who for?'

Warmed by the inner glow his words evoked, she broke road rules and laid her hand on his thigh. Felt him tense and his muscle contract. For a fleeting moment, his hand covered hers then returned to the wheel.

Jack gritted his teeth, kept his mind on the road and tried not to think about the heat spreading from Cassie's hand. His chest felt tight and his pulse was faster than the ute's speedo. Legally, he ought to ask her to remove her hold but the words stuck in his throat. Wouldn't make a difference; its mark would last longer than the trip home.

He knew she was nervous. Her tension filled the cabin but this wasn't the time or place to tell her she had only committed to dinner with him. When they were face to face, he'd convince her that *when* they made love wasn't as important as her not having a skerrick of doubt it was right for them.

Her features appeared calm every time he glanced her way, though he never caught her looking at him. Her breathing was regular, and her fingers lay still on his leg. No way did he want to disturb her when he couldn't hold her in his arms.

He'd slowed down, activating the roller door as he turned into his driveway. Before the engine had fully died, he turned to her and cupped her face in his hands. Her skin was warm, her eyes were soft and inviting, and he was human flesh and blood.

'Cassie, the evening's yours. The table's set, and the meal's ready to be cooked. We can eat, talk and watch TV and I'll take you home whenever you say. I'm happy just to be with you, see you smile and hear you laugh.'

'Thank you, Jack.' Polite and mundane when he wanted breathless and passionate.

With every kilometre, Cassie's insecurities had grown and she'd become a ball of taut muscles and cold, churning insides. Unable to face him, she'd had no choice when he'd turned her head towards him. His hands were warm and protective on her skin, and the desire burning in his bright green eyes wrapped around her like a cocoon.

She heard her bland reply, and cringed inside as the flame dimmed.

Forget the meal. I want to taste you on my lips much more than I want to taste your cooking. Coward—say it out loud. Tell him.

'Hmm. Let's go inside.' He brushed a feather kiss on her mouth, backed away and opened his door. Jerked back, and burst out laughing.

'Taking off my seatbelt might help.'

In a heartbeat, her mind cleared. All reservations and

fears for the future were swamped by a wave of longing so powerful it stole the breath from her body. As long as he wanted her, she was his.

She laughed with him and slid from her seat to meet him as he came round the bonnet. He held her hand as he ushered her through the door and laundry into the hall. She stopped him there, rose up on her toes and kissed him.

'Take me to bed now, Jack. Please.'

Startled eyes stared into hers for the few seconds it took for her words to sink in. Then he swung her up into his arms and strode towards the stairs.

'Any time you want, my darling Cassie.'

A week later, Cassie stood in Mel's dining room staring at the empty plate in her hand, unsure what had happened to the sandwich she'd made for her lunch. She walked back to the kitchen, berating herself for the umpteenth time for daydreaming.

It was all due to Jack. A week ago, she'd returned from their walk on the beach, facing the enticing probability of becoming his lover. Since then they'd been together every evening, except Saturday when she'd been at home catching up with her friends and personal stuff.

The mere act of closing her eyes transported her in her mind to his bed or that wide, extra-long sofa where she'd experienced pleasure beyond anything she'd believed existed. He'd made love to her with a tenderness and devotion that quelled any remaining qualms the first time and deepened her adoration for him with unbelievable passion every time after.

She quivered at the memory of his eyes hot with desire, his gentle hands arousing her, and his kisses urging her higher until she touched the stars. She'd never be the same again, never be able to look at any other man without comparing him to Jack. This might mean she'd be alone for the rest of her life but she'd never regret a moment.

Her phone rang, ending her reverie. She ran to the family room where she'd left it, felt her stomach dip as she sighted Val's ID instead of Jack's.

'Hi, Cassie! Mel called to say Janette had a healthy little boy. Ten days early and both are well so they might go home in a couple of days. I'll organise a party to celebrate when Mel comes home and you're invited.'

Neither she nor Jack had told anyone of their affair. For her it was too special, too intimate to share, even with Narelle. Now, with the prospect of Mel being home soon, she wondered how much longer it would last.

They chatted for a while and Val promised to pop in for coffee on Friday before saying goodbye.

What did a party mean to them? Adults only or children included? At someone's home or an upmarket restaurant? Casual or formal dress?

Too many questions she had no answer for. She'd ask Jack tonight.

Her warm glow returned. She found her sandwich, poured a glass of water and went to the sunroom to daydream about this evening while she ate.

CHAPTER FIFTEEN

THE FOLLOWING MORNING, Cassie worked in the dining room accompanied by continuous rain on the roof. She walked Sam during a clear break before lunch, then continued.

Mid-afternoon, she took her coffee and the paperback she'd bought on impulse into the sunroom, her favourite in the house. This was a place for solitude or shared confidences, not like the other areas which resonated with echoes of family get-togethers and boisterous laughter.

Curling up in the comfy old chair by the window was like being back in the house she'd grown up in, warm and inviting. She could reminisce about happy times with only a gentle twinge of regret.

She wriggled back, sipped her stimulating drink and lost herself in the story of two brothers and a sister fighting the elements for the survival of their family's cattle ranch in southern Queensland.

Totally engrossed, it took a moment or two for it to register that the soothing classical music had stopped. She went to the lounge to check the sound system. No red light, no response to turning it on and off. A job for Jack.

Walking into the hall, she became aware of the silence. Where was the hum of the fridge and freezer from the kitchen? She clicked the nearest wall switch. Nothing, which probably meant a short power outage. Not surprising considering the torrential rain.

First thing: check the switchboard on the side wall of the house. Coat on and umbrella out, she walked out into the downpour, Sam at her heels. All the circuit breakers were in the on position, so she went down the driveway and looked both ways. She couldn't see any lights but that didn't help as few people would be home at this time.

She ran back inside, followed by a reluctant Sam who wanted to play in the rain. Because Mel's landline was out, she called the utility company on her mobile, and got bleeps. If their helpline had been inundated, it might mean the problem wasn't limited to the immediate area.

She'd just have to wait and trust it was easily fixed. To be on the safe side, she unplugged the rechargeable torch in the laundry, found the smaller one and spare batteries in the kitchen drawer, and took them to the sunroom. Settling into the chair, she finished her coffee and resumed reading.

It wasn't the same. Going over the same half page twice without taking any of it in was wasting time. She couldn't dismiss the world around her or force her concentration to block it out. She sat thinking, acutely aware of every vehicle that passed the house, the closed book on her lap.

Jack had mentioned his two customers for today lived on opposite sides of the city, and hopefully neither had been affected. Calling him would seem like she was panicking, while he was always cool and level-headed. It hadn't been long and the emergency crews would be stretched today.

She jumped and scrambled for her mobile when it rang, holding her breath. It whooshed out at the sight of his ID on her screen.

'Jack, I was thinking…'

'Are you home? Are you okay?' Rasped out as if *he* were alarmed.

'Yes, to both. We've lost power but…'

His sigh of relief was audible. 'Everyone has, darling. The whole damn state is out, including all traffic lights. Might not be back on until tomorrow. I'm stuck out north, and driving home's going to be a nightmare.'

'Oh.' Her first thoughts of no lights or heating became

instantly insignificant. 'Perhaps you should stay somewhere and come home tomorrow.'

'No way.' Ground out into her ear, its message warmed her better than any domestic heater.

'I have to tidy up this job then I'll come for you and Sam. Conserve your mobile battery, use it only if you have to, and pack an overnight bag. Take care, and wrap up warm, darling. I'll call you when I'm on my way.'

'You too, Jack.'

She switched off, and let her hand holding the phone fall into her lap. The whole state? Until tomorrow? Her mind struggled to grasp the enormity of the situation.

Everyone was reliant on constant electricity, and tended to get annoyed at any loss. They'd be unprepared and frustrated, especially as their mobiles ran out of battery, even more exasperated as they tried to get home in peak traffic.

Jack would be caught up in the turmoil. She didn't want to think of it, needed to keep busy. Her shivering might be from the cold creeping into the now unheated house or from worry about him. Or both. Collecting her notebook and pen from the family room, she went upstairs, taking one torch and her mobile with her.

When she began to pack her airline carry-on bag, she realised what she'd tacitly agreed to. She was going to spend the night with him. In his bed or one of the guestrooms? If he asked, was she ready to literally sleep with him? She selected her favourite pale green and lace nightie. In case she decided she was.

That task finished, she went from room to room, checking power points and switches, making a note of the appliances she unplugged or left as they were. The house was now dim and shadowy, eerie without the usual streetlights shining in.

She huddled in Bob's big armchair where Jack usually sat, wearing her warmest coat and wrapped in a quilt,

Sam curled up nearby. Holding her mobile in her hand, she willed Jack to call.

Even though he'd told her to save the battery, she accessed her photo file on her mobile. She needed a diversion to prevent herself from thinking about him out there in the chaos, and Mum's smiling face raised her spirits. She'd handled everything life had thrown her way with faith and patience. Cassie smiled as memories came flooding back with each picture.

Her ringtone was startlingly loud in the totally silent house, and Jack didn't give her a chance to speak.

'Cassie? I'm less than twenty minutes away. Are you ready?'

'Yes, but…'

'Tell me when I get there.'

Jack hung up, not giving her a chance to voice whatever doubts she might have conceived sitting alone in the dark. He'd been on edge since he'd accessed the power company's website and read their prediction.

The unit he was doing repairs at was his second furthest property from home and, for the first time ever, he regretted the distance. Normally he preferred distance between his working and his personal life.

He had made sure everything was safe before he'd left, knowing he'd have to return and have it ready for the young couple due to move in on the weekend. At least Cassie was safe at home, and had sounded confident and composed.

Keeping calm as he negotiated his way home was easier than he'd expected because most drivers understood the situation, were patient and applied good road rules. And once people got home, they'd stay there. Shops, restaurants and other venues were all closed, unless they had back-up generators.

Even so, the journey took twice as long, the rain didn't

stop, and the churning in his stomach morphed into fear. He wanted, needed to see Cassie, hold and kiss her. Feel her warm and safe in his embrace.

His anxiety eased as he pulled up in Mel's driveway and jumped from the ute. Sprinting round to the back door and up the steps, he was in time to have a bright beam shine in his eyes. He skidded to a halt, blood pumping, chest heaving and heart pounding.

Sam pushed past the dim figure holding the torch, and Jack brushed his ears as he strode forward. No words were needed. He drew Cassie as close as humanly possible and buried his head into her silken hair. She felt soft and warm, smelt sweet and enticing, and was where she belonged.

She clung to him and he murmured words of comfort, ignoring the torch pressing into his spine, macho pride surging as her trembling subsided.

'I'm here, darling. You're safe. Everything's okay.' He'd have been content to stay this way longer but the need to have her warm was his first priority.

Then she raised her head and everything was forgotten except the desire to kiss her now. He trailed light touches from her forehead to her mouth and settled, tightening his grip at the sound of her sigh. The rain, the storms, the blackout—nothing intruded into the magic world of her lips responding to his.

Woof. Sam broke the spell, letting them know he was there.

Cassie pulled away and shone the torch towards the dog.

'I think he wants to get warm. Me too.' In truth, she was burning inside from his kiss, couldn't wait for more.

'Well, let's go. Where's your bag?'

'Just inside. I've checked…'

'Tell me on the way.' He was already pushing open the

screen door. His being brusque shouldn't thrill her, yet it proved how anxious he'd been.

Sam followed as she guided their path to his ute then put the torch on the floor at her feet. It felt surreal, driving in the rain through suburban streets at night with the only illumination coming from their headlights. Occasionally there'd be another vehicle, keeping a moderate speed as they were.

No power meant leaving the ute in the driveway while they entered through the front door. Jack sent her to the lounge, and ran upstairs for blankets. She stayed there for a few minutes then went to find him, setting up on the canopy-protected patio. Wherever he was, she wanted to be.

'Stubborn creature.' His frown and gruff tone when she walked out was negated by his short, firm kiss.

Settling into a folding chair, she admired his expertise that had the barbecue fired up and the patio heater glowing within minutes. When Sam joined them, Jack brought out his bed.

'To him, a barbecue means food,' he said as he set it next to Cassie. 'And kids, and games, and stealing scraps from under chairs.'

The rain eased as the steak and sausages sizzled. Water boiled on a small camping stove, providing hot chocolate for her and coffee for him. Cassie sighed wistfully, thinking of her Outback fantasy. As quiet as she was, Jack heard, stopped turning the food and looked up.

'Cassie?'

She had to give a reason and, to her, fudging wasn't lying.

'I have this image in my head of camping far from any town where the lighting effects the sky. There's a big, bright moon and millions of stars, and no other people around.'

Except you.

He chuckled. And there it was, startlingly real in her mind.

'Sounds a bit solitary to me. Apart from having company, I like it. We don't get away as much as we used to. Work, marriage and kids take precedence, as they should.'

And she'd bet there'd been plenty of girls willing to go along.

Once they'd eaten, he refused help cleaning up and shooed her inside. She curled up in the corner of his long lounge, flicking through phrases in her mind. She'd never been forward with men, didn't know how to be.

She was still undecided when he knelt in front of her.

'It's twenty past eight. Feels much later because it's so dark. You want…?'

'To sleep in your arms, Jack.'

He didn't need to be told twice. He scooped her up, blanket and all, and was heading up the stairs before she'd taken a breath.

Sam's cold nose on Jack's bare shoulder made him shiver. He stirred, waved a hand and told Sam to go settle. He went with reluctance.

Waking a little more, Jack became aware of the soft form nestled into his, and his lips curved. Cassie was here. Their lovemaking had been incredible and she'd stayed. A gigantic positive in the blackout.

He caressed her silken skin, relishing the way she wriggled in response, and opened his eyes. His own sleeping beauty, and he could see her clearly in the light from the hall.

The power was back. He checked his alarm clock on the bedside cabinet. Nine twenty-seven. The repair crews had worked wonders, considering the extent of the failure.

He brushed a finger across Cassie's lips. She blinked, her smile reigniting the heat that had barely died down.

'Hi.' Sleep-husky and sexy as hell.

'Hi, yourself. Anyone ever tell you how sweet you look when you're asleep?'

'No.' She blinked again. 'I can see you.'

'Mmm, and it's only nine-thirty.'

She snuggled closer. 'Better go back to sleep then.'

His heart pounded, sending his pulse into overdrive. She didn't want to be taken home. Hot prickles shot through his body, bringing it fully awake.

He cupped the back of her neck and kissed her with all the passion flooding through him.

'I've got a better idea. We can sleep later.'

Her slow, sleepy-eyed sensual smile told him it would be much later.

Late Saturday evening, Jack drove her home after a day spent at his house. He unbuckled his seatbelt, and pulled Cassie into his arms. She returned his kiss with ardour, knowing they'd have to behave with more discretion from tomorrow when Mel arrived home.

She'd told no one they were lovers because she was convinced it was never meant to last. They hadn't discussed it, and there'd been no hint from his relatives so she assumed he hadn't told anyone either.

'Do you have any idea what you do to me?' His rough words and breathy tone were a pretty good indication. She could arouse him with a smile, a touch or a kiss. And that was all it could ever be.

He ran the back of his fingers across her cheek, kissed the tip of her nose when she trembled. 'When are we going to be together again?'

Tomorrow, but he meant in his bed.

'We can't while I'm here with Mel. I... I couldn't.'

'I'll wait, but not willingly. I want you, Cassie, more than anything else in my life.'

He kissed her again, showing her how much, before forcing himself away with a throaty growl. His farewell at the back door was gentle, reverent. Its effect just as shattering. Every day she cared a little more; every moment with him was going to make the parting more painful.

She had coffee and scones ready when Jack brought Mel home from the airport the next morning. She hoped she'd be forgiven for using a packet mix by serving them warm from the oven with fresh cream and raspberry jam.

Sam was panting with excitement, his tail whipping up a wind storm behind him when he saw Mel. After greeting him with enthusiasm, she hugged Cassie, kissed her cheek and handed her a small gift bag.

'Just a little something from Melbourne as a thank you.'

The *little something* was a sheer white scarf exquisitely decorated with blue roses and pale green petals.

'It's beautiful, Mel.' She blinked back the tears threatening to form and hugged her employer back. 'Thank you. I love it.'

'I'm the one who owes *you* gratitude. Because you were here, I got to hold my first great-grandchild when he was less than an hour old. He's gorgeous, so tiny and so perfect. Let's sit in the lounge. I've got lots of photos on my phone to show you.'

Cassie carried the tray with the drinks, and Jack took Mel's suitcases to her room before joining them. Mel sat in the middle, eagerly scrolling from photo to photo and giving a commentary of each one.

Cassie made appropriate noises and kept her gaze on the screen to hide the envy she knew would show in her eyes. She'd been shocked by the leaden grip that had formed in her stomach at the first sight of the baby. Had never been jealous of motherhood before.

'He's adorable. I'm happy for them. My best friend's

second baby is due in early December and they can't wait.
I'm excited too.'

She spoke the truth, and she hadn't felt the slightest bit
jealous of them having her godson or his soon-to-be sibling. Until now.

'Do you want some of those snaps printed out for Val's
cocktail party tonight, Mel?' Jack asked, and Cassie's answer exploded in her head.

He was the difference. She'd never pictured any of the
men she'd previously met as daddy figures, hadn't thought
of Jack that way either. Until now. Her heart obviously
wasn't in sync with her head.

'Yes, please, Jack. I'm looking forward to it. You're coming with us, aren't you, Cassie?'

A frantic refocus, and she was able to answer calmly.
'Yes, Val kindly invited me.'

'I'd be taking you anyway. I'll rest this afternoon, don't
want to fall asleep during the fun.' She turned off her
phone, put it on the table and lifted her cup.

'I'll get the scones.' Cassie stood and left the room, waiting until she reached the kitchen before huffing the breath
from her lungs.

Jack watched her walk out, attuned to her mood, noting
her quick pace and the set of her shoulders. Why had the
photos upset her? One of the secrets in her past? Someday
soon he'd take her somewhere quiet where they wouldn't
be disturbed and find out. It was time he came clean with
his own secret, time he changed his vision of the future.

CHAPTER SIXTEEN

MEL WAS RESTED and waiting in the lounge when Jack arrived to pick them up, intending to find time tonight to speak to Cassie alone. The phone call he'd received this afternoon meant he'd be catching an early flight in the morning.

The final meeting. Minor details sorted and the documents would be signed. Time away to sort out why and how his future plans had changed, and how much he wanted Cassie to be a part of them. Time away where her touch, her smile, her very essence couldn't addle his mind and confound his logic.

'You look fabulous, Mel.' He hugged her and kissed her cheek. 'We might even get to have that dance tonight.'

'Flatterer. You don't look too bad yourself. I haven't seen you in a suit for a while.'

'It's likely to become my day-to-day wear all too soon. I…'

Words failed him. His throat was dry as a sandstorm, and he'd swear his heart stopped before slamming into his rib cage then racing as if turbocharged.

Cassie as he'd never seen her, stealing his breath and fuelling his libido, stood in the doorway. He'd seen a 'little black dress' on so many women but it had never had such an effect, had never looked so incredible. It enhanced every sweet curve he knew intimately, and the deceptively simple set of matching silver jewellery suited her to perfection.

From her shining black hair, all the way down her enticing body and shapely legs, to black high-heeled shoes, she was deliciously, delightfully exquisite. A burning desire to whisk her away to his home and rekindle the heat that sparked with every kiss or touch flared in every cell in his body.

Moving towards her, he became aware of hesitation in her usually bright eyes, and in her stance. Others might not notice her slight body quiver, or the tight grip on her small black clutch bag. For him, every nuance was part of the make-up of a special woman who'd slipped through his defences, causing him to re-evaluate his life expectations.

He inhaled her fragrance of peach and sensual woman, took her hands in his and kissed each one, surprised by how cold they were. His pulse hitched as her eyes softened, and her lips parted.

'You are absolutely stunning, Cassie. Forget your nerves. Everyone's looking forward to seeing you.'

Mel backed him up. 'He's right, dear. You look beautiful and it's a small, adults-only family night. Relax and you'll have a good time. I'll get my wrap.'

She walked out and Jack took the opportunity to tip Cassie's chin up and press a quick kiss on her delectable mouth. Found himself fighting the urge to wrap his arms around her and deepen the kiss, have her melt into him. Felt empty as she held up her hand and stepped away.

'Do any of them know about us?' She spoke quietly, her head held high, and he flicked a glance towards the door.

'No.' He bent his head, not wanting Mel to hear, cupped Cassie's cheek and brushed his thumb over her lips. 'I'd like to keep it that way a little longer. Trust me, Cassie.'

Trust him? Cassie was drowning in a sea of contradictions. Starting with the man in front of her, so different to the everyday guy who'd charmed her with breakfast, walks on the beach and laughter.

She'd formed pictures in her mind of how he'd look in formal wear. They'd come nowhere near this debonair macho male, muscles defined in a dark tailored suit, white shirt with silver sheen and green tie matching his hypnotic eyes. Even his unruly brown hair fitted the image.

It seemed as if he couldn't keep his hands off her if they were alone, but hardly touched her in the presence of people he knew. He showered her with compliments every day and passionate erotic phrases as they made love but never spoke of the future, didn't want their relationship known to anyone. She'd heard his comment about the suit. It could only mean he was planning a corporate career.

Being with him made her feel so alive, as if the world was hers for the taking. When they were apart, the reality of the chasm between them slammed home. This cocktail party was a new scene altogether, a chance to show his family he was attracted to her. He'd decided not to take it.

Cassie's trepidation shot skyward as they entered the picture-perfect gardens of a designer-built, exclusive family home overlooking the city. Ultra-modern with the central area two storeys high, everything inside and out had been selected with taste, and no expense spared. It appeared that Val's favourite colours were muted greens and blues with bold splashes of red.

Entering the long reception room, complete with built-in bar and grand piano, overlooking a paved patio and swimming pool, was like walking onto the set of a movie. She'd been introduced to and hugged by so many people she'd lost count. *Small family night, huh.*

The trays of food set out on scattered tables were replenished frequently during the evening. Seats and armchairs had been placed in groups, allowing guests to sit and chat in private.

Confident as far as her appearance went, she was acutely conscious of the gulf between her standing in life and his family's natural acceptance of their wealth and position.

Yet they gave no indication at all that she was in any way not their social equal.

Four of Jack's female first and second cousins invited her to sit with them, their initial conversation about the upcoming finale of a top-rating reality series. Then somehow they moved on to opinions of other guests' apparel, never nasty, mostly complimentary. She listened without comment.

'Jack's looking particularly elegant tonight,' Silvia—or was it Silvana?—observed. 'Is that a new suit? He'll need it if he ends up being the CEO of a chain of shopping centres.'

'Shh, we're not supposed to know.' The girl next to her tapped her hand. 'It's very hush-hush until the initial deal's signed off.'

'I can't picture him behind a desk every day. I thought he'd dropped the idea.'

Cassie's stomach sank lower with every word. He'd talked with such enthusiasm about gardening and his repair and maintenance work—how he enjoyed being outside. Had it all been a sham?

She took a mouthful of her ice-cold drink, and glanced across the room to where he stood with Val, her husband and another couple. One second was all it needed to raise her pulse and stir an aching need in her core.

Tall, handsome and self-assured, seemingly without a care in the world, his personality dominated the group. Dominated the room. Dominated her life.

He turned his head towards her and she dropped hers, raising her glass to her lips. She concentrated on the woman beside her as she talked of her son's escapades.

A waitress offered them a choice from a tray of hors d'oeuvres and she selected blindly. For her it was tasteless. Another brought wine. She emptied her glass and asked for water.

'How's Mel's sorting going, Cassie? Becoming a great-grandmother and offloading unwanted stuff has really boosted her spirits. We're all grateful for your help.'

It was easy to return the compliment with a genuine smile. They were nice people; she just wasn't in their league.

She mixed with other groups, ensuring she was not in eyeline with Jack if he was included. Later Val turned up the music and her husband claimed Cassie for a dance as Jack whirled Mel around the floor as promised. After a second one with a cousin, she sat watching, claiming truthfully she had a slight headache whenever asked. Jack never offered.

They were the first to leave due to Mel feeling tired, and more hugs and kisses made for a drawn-out goodbye. Cassie climbed into the back of the cabin and slumped against the seat.

'Tired, Cassie? It's been a long day for both of you.'

She was weary, apprehensive and her nerves were frayed. Her head throbbed and her heart hurt, the pain deepening at the apparent genuine concern in his eyes as they met hers in the rear-vision mirror. He'd shown none while they'd been with his family.

'Yes, I think I'll go straight to bed.'

He frowned, glanced towards Mel and firmed his lips.

'Sleep's a good idea for you both. Did you enjoy the evening?' Why the hard edge to his voice?

'It was very memorable. You are lucky to have such a close family.'

'Something I don't take for granted, never will.'

'Me neither,' Mel chipped in. 'Every single one of them is precious to me.'

Jack swung out of the parking space, his main focus on the driving, his peripheral thoughts on Cassie, and his gut churning. He knew she was upset, and wasn't sure if it

was because she'd heard something or because of his behaviour. He'd fought with himself all night about keeping
distance from her.

There was no way he could have been close or danced
with her without the attraction being obvious to everyone
there. He cared—more than cared—but still had lingering
doubts about his past, and his ability to sustain such an intense relationship without reverting to temper outbursts.

Cassie had hidden issues too. He'd sensed her reluctance
to become involved from the day they'd met. Now she'd
skittled his plan to talk to her alone after Mel went to bed.
Not that he'd have told her much, couldn't until everything
was signed and sealed.

'I received a call this afternoon. I'll be flying to Sydney
first thing tomorrow, not sure for how long.'

His gaze flicked to Cassie in the mirror. She swung towards the window —not fast enough for him to miss the
pain sweeping across her face and the quick intake of air.

Hell, he wished he had more time. This was the culmi-
nation of a plan dreamt of in his teens, and worked towards
since. He knew exactly what he was doing, just wasn't certain about explaining the life changes to others.

'I have no idea when or if I'll have time to call.'

'We understand,' Mel said then closed her eyes and let
her head fall back.

The smooth purr of the engine evoked the memory of
driving home the first night he and Cassie made love. She'd
been sweet and loving, shy, and yet sexier than any woman
he'd ever known. His own beautiful enigma.

He glanced at the mirror again. *His. His Cassie.* The
phrase echoed in his head for the rest of the drive.

At the house, he told Mel to wait, stepped out by Cassie's
already opening door and strode round it to catch her arm
as she slid out. She didn't look up until he growled in frustration, and bent his head to her ear.

'Trust me, Cassie. Please.'

She trembled and he pulled her tight against him, brushed his lips on her forehead then released her.

'Please.' Her wide sad eyes tore at his heart.

She nodded and slipped past him to go to Mel. He followed and helped his aunt down, hugging and kissing her. Once they were safe inside, he headed home for a restless night.

Mel persuaded Cassie to go home on Tuesday afternoon, claiming she hadn't seemed well the last two days. Hugging her before she left, Mel urged her to see a doctor if she didn't feel better in a day or so.

Cassie doubted she ever would. Jack hadn't phoned her, and his calls to Mel had been rushed, with excuses of long meetings and no mention of when he'd be home.

Keeping their involvement a secret from his aunt and family was proof it was purely physical on his part. That had been her initial desire too, only now she found she wanted more than he was able to give.

She drove slowly, her thoughts intruding into her concentration on the road, and she almost missed the amber light turning red.

She realised she'd been mentally preparing herself for an *I'm sorry but* speech since their very first kiss. His upbringing and innate honour ensured he'd do it in person, and she'd accept his excuses with as much grace as she could muster and let him walk away. The affair had been of her choosing and she'd never regret a moment in his arms.

Her mindset had subtly changed as her initial attraction deepened and blossomed into love. Now she…

She started as a horn sounded behind her. Giving a wave of apology, she drove off and determinedly blocked Jack out until she reached home. Leaving her luggage unpacked in her room, she went for a walk to think.

'Trust me,' he'd said. Trust him to let her down gently so he could devote his time to his new corporate venture? She loved him. Hearing him mouth platitudes and wish her the best was going to shatter her. Losing control and crying would be embarrassing for him and mortifying for her.

What if she ended it first? Let him walk away with no guilt? His pride might be dented a little but he'd bounce back. For him there was no emotional tie, only, as he'd said, an incredible physical experience.

She meandered aimlessly, her mind searching for and rehearsing the words that would tear her heart in two. Not wanting the stomach-churning anticipation to last any longer than necessary, and definitely not being brave enough for a personal confrontation, she texted him.

Please phone me as soon as possible.

It was not how Mum had taught her to behave, but if he was there his sandalwood aroma would stir her senses, his intoxicating green eyes would cloud her judgement. She'd stumble over her words, stop and start, and completely mess up. If he asked why in his deep smooth voice that tingled her spine, she'd have no answer that she was willing to give.

He rang sooner than she expected but then she'd never have been ready. She picked up her mobile, sat on her bed, stood up and sat again. Her finger trembled as she swiped to receive.

'Cassie, is there something wrong? I've got ten minutes. Can it wait until I get home?'

He sounded hassled, making her feel guilty. Then she hardened her heart. Being hassled was par for the course for an executive of an expanding business; he'd better get used to it.

'No. I can't see you then.'

'What? Are you going somewhere?'

'I don't want to see you again.'

The line went silent. She pictured his face, brow furrowed over darkening eyes, lips parted and hand rubbing his neck as he stretched from sitting too long. There was the sound of a long exhalation of breath.

'You picked a hell of a time to tell me. Do you want to explain?' Harsh and barely contained.

'I can't. It's the right course…the right thing for everyone.'

Please, please hang up before I break down.

'And I don't get a say in the decision?'

'There's no other option. Please respect my decision. Goodbye, Jack.'

She hung up, put her mobile on silent and hid it in her wardrobe. Collapsing onto her bed, she could no longer hold back the tears. She loved him, and she'd set him free to find someone who'd fit the image of a perfect executive's wife. They'd have a fabulous house and adorable children, and she'd…she'd never stop loving him. She sobbed until her pillow was soaked and her throat raw.

Fourteen hundred kilometres away, in a high-rise office block on Sydney's North Shore, Jack stared at his phone in disbelief. She'd dumped him. Refused to explain.

Anger simmered below the amazement. But he'd be damned if he'd accept it without her telling him why to his face. They were incredible together, perfectly tuned to each other's desires. She was his, had been from the moment she'd asked him to take her to bed. Hell, he'd screwed up. He should have told her how he felt.

'Jack?'

He swung round, pocketing his phone. To heck with dotting every 'i'. They'd work late tonight, and tomorrow they'd sign off on the main points. The peripheral stuff could be agreed by email or at a future meeting.

He had business at home to deal with.

* * *

Jack's flight landed in Adelaide a few minutes early on Wednesday evening. By six-thirty he'd picked up his ute from long-term parking, and made a quick call to Mel, felt relieved when *she* mentioned Cassie first.

'Cassie hasn't been feeling well since Sunday so I sent her home yesterday. Hopefully a few days' rest is all she needs.'

'I'm sure she'll be fine. She's resilient. You take care, Mel. I'll see you tomorrow.'

He parked in the last street space available, half a block from Cassie's home. His throat felt dry and raw, his gut churned and his brain felt overloaded from trying to work out *why?* What if she wouldn't listen to him, wouldn't see him…? No, not to be contemplated.

He swiped his hand across his mouth, jumped from the ute and strode to her front door. There was no sound inside, no sign of life. He didn't have a plan B so he'd wait on the porch until someone came.

Sending up a silent prayer, he rang the doorbell. A door slammed, a male voice called out 'Coming', and something heavy thumped on the floor inside.

He sucked in air and waited. Whatever he'd expected, it wasn't the blond, well-built athlete who, hand on the half-open door, studied him with guarded interest.

'Yeah?'

Jack pulled the flyscreen door open. 'Is Cassie home?'

'Who wants to know?' Was his blunt demand a friend's protection for her or something more?

'Jack Randell.' He hoped it sounded more confident to the man confronting him than it felt, and automatically straightened his shoulders as he was subjected to the most intense scrutiny he could ever remember enduring. Determinedly keeping steady eye contact, he refused to buckle, wouldn't leave until he'd seen her.

With a slight nod of the head, the guardian of the door pushed it wide open and held out his hand.

'Brad Collins. *Cassie's friend and housemate.*' Jack heard the message, wasn't sure it meant he was confirming that was all they were or sending him a warning.

His surprise must have been evident as he returned the firm handshake because Brad's eyebrows rose for a second and he grinned.

'She didn't tell you she shared with two guys? Interesting. Come on in.'

Two guys? Jack was still trying to process that fact as he entered a spacious lounge area and nearly tripped over a large gym bag. His mishap amused Brad even more, though there was no malice in the short laugh.

A toot from outside turned both heads. Brad caught the flyscreen, preventing it from closing, and waved at the blue car pulling into the driveway. 'Be right there.' He walked across the lounge and disappeared into the hallway.

Jack heard a loud double knock on wood then, 'Cassie, you got a minute?'

Not waiting for an answer, Brad returned, swung his bag over his shoulder and picked up a set of keys from the coffee table. His eyes locked with Jack's and the tacit message was strong and unmistakable.

Hurt her anymore and you'll answer to me.

He nodded, still stunned that Cassie had omitted to mention that her housemates were male, yet thankful that she had such a champion, and that the man trusted him enough to leave them alone.

After a short pause, Brad gave a quick echoing gesture and left, closing both doors behind him. Leaving Jack alone to face the challenge of his life.

CHAPTER SEVENTEEN

JACK STOOD, EYES focused on that doorway, every muscle tensed, every cell in his body attuned to the soft footsteps coming nearer. He drew breath and held it, his mouth dried and his hands splayed on his thighs.

Suddenly she was there, framed in the doorway, his gorgeous, sunny, beloved Cassie... Except...?

He felt his heart rupture, painfully ripping apart, and he'd swear it would leave a permanent scar.

Her usually beautiful, sparkling brown eyes were dulled, rimmed with shadows, and her sweet, quirky lips gave no welcome. She looked tired and broken and he couldn't fathom what the hell he'd done to cause such anguish.

'Cassie?' Raspy. Fractured. Like he felt.

She gasped, startled by his presence. Her eyes grew larger, darker, a bright red flush appeared on her cheeks, emphasising her pallor, and her hands flew to clamp round her waist. Her head swung towards the dining area past the front door, as if seeking support.

'Brad left.'

No way would he be following her friend until he'd found out why she'd dumped him. On the damn phone. He tried to suppress the niggling irritation and had to admit defeat. It simmered in his gut, more so now he'd seen its effect on her.

She swallowed, drawing his eyes to the slight movement of her throat.

'I said I didn't want to see you.' He hadn't believed her then, didn't now. There was a yearning in her tone that tugged at his heartstrings, gave him the tiniest glimmer of hope.

'I heard. I want to know why. After what we shared, I deserve that much consideration.'

She held his gaze for so long he was on the point of marching over, taking her into his arms and kissing her. He was positive deep down to his soul that she cared for him, so why the charade? Even now he could see desire—for him—ignite, bringing a faint glow to her lacklustre eyes. One gentle kiss and he wouldn't be able to stop until she melted into him as she always did, alleviating his anguish.

Her sudden blink and quick headshake broke the spell. She took careful steps to an old round-armed chair and sank into its well-worn cushions. He frowned as she drew her legs up and wrapped her arms around her body, as if needing protection. From him?

Scouring his mind for a reason for her apprehension, he sat in the chair on the other side of the fireplace, giving her space. Clasping his hands between his legs and leaning forward, he waited.

The tip of her tongue appeared, and ran across her lip line, nearly tipping him over the edge. Did she have any idea how provocative her action was?

Staying calm was the best way of getting an answer so he dug deep for the self-discipline he'd been so proud of. He wasn't completely successful. Watching her breasts rise and fall in agitation had him fisting his hands, shifting in his seat and digging even deeper.

Cassie hugged her stomach tighter. Jack was here. In her home, asking—no, demanding—an explanation. His male ego must have brought him; limited truth would send him away.

'You. Your family. Your social position and lifestyle.

I don't fit.' Even to her ears it sounded lame. She flicked her hand, encompassing the room. 'I can't live that way.'

Her words made no impression. If anything, he seemed to find them irrelevant. He ground out an oath, one she'd never have expected him to use in any situation.

Her jaw dropped, her head jerked, and a gleam appeared in his green eyes. His sharp bark of laughter cut through the air and its irony had no magic to conjure up her Outback daydream.

'If I believed that for one second, Cassie Clarkson, I'd never have kissed you, no matter how attractive I found you.'

She fought back. 'Your whole family socialise with the elite of Adelaide—Australia, even. You're invited to gala events people like me would need a police check to attend as a waitress.'

Seeing his brow furrow and his eyes narrow, she realised she'd hit a nerve, and her stomach clenched. She wanted, desperately needed, to be alone. Before she broke down and admitted she ached to be in his arms, held close and cherished, his lips kissing away all thoughts of separation. Her head ached, her brain was a foggy mess and she spoke without thinking.

'You're so much more than you divulge to the world.'

He took a deep breath and squared his shoulders. She continued, not giving him a chance to butt in.

'And your new enterprise will take you a giant step further up the corporate ladder.'

His eyebrow shot upwards then his features froze. 'Enterprise? Whose gossip have you been listening to, Cassie?'

He pronounced the words with care, voice flat and devoid of its richness, his eyes as hard as granite. His scornful *huff* hung in the air as he continued. 'Of course, you hear things. I seem to remember you saying you don't retain them.'

'You're not denying it. You kept your corporate ambitions well hidden; now they'll make you super rich and...'

He cut in, restraint abandoned, anger rising. 'And you're not prepared to talk this out, try to find out where what we have might lead? That's not the impression I got from our time together.'

She stared in disbelief at the agitated stranger in front of her, so different to the disciplined Jack she knew. It was as if he were keeping a mere semblance of control by the barest of threads.

She wouldn't cave in. She mustn't. For his sake. Because she loved him more than life itself. Focusing on what was best for him, she ignored the throbbing in her head.

'That's not for me. It's better we split now. Move on with no regrets.'

He lunged to his feet, sending her shrinking into the cushions. A second later a surge of adrenaline sent her upright, facing him with her head held high, determined to negate any argument. Without conscious thought, she narrowed the gap between them a little.

'Move on?' He flung his arms out wide as if to encompass the world. The vein in his forehead pulsed, the corner of his mouth twitched, and his eyes pinned her with scorn. His resentment hung in the air, almost tangible. Surrounding her.

This was a side to him she'd never have imagined, so far removed from the restraint he'd always exercised. Because she'd made the decision, not him?

'That's your future plan? To discard everything we shared—the walks, the kisses?' His Adam's apple jerked in his throat. 'Making love?'

She began to quiver inside as his voice rose with every word, the last two rough and raspy as if painful to get out. Yet she didn't retreat, strangely felt no sense of danger.

He stepped towards her. 'You're suggesting we move on

to someone else, Cassie? Date *them*? Kiss *them*? Make love to *them*?' Each emphasis cut deep, as he intended.

Another step and he loomed over her, green eyes blazing. 'Tell me how the hell I'm supposed to do that when I'm so totally crazily in love with *you.'*

No. No, he couldn't be—mustn't be. Obviously didn't want to be. Her world spun into orbit, leaving her disorientated and gasping for air. Holding up her hand in denial, she backed away until her legs hit the armchair.

'No. No, Jack, I… Please. It…it's…'

Words failed her as the colour drained from Jack's face and his features contorted. His head shook from side to side in slow motion, his fingers clenched then splayed and his eyes glazed over as if he were seeing another time, another place.

'Don't…don't go. I'm sorry. Please. Don't go.' His faltering voice, and the ragged pain in his voice stunned her.

Go? Go where?

A violent shudder ran through him; he staggered back and sank into the chair he'd vacated minutes earlier. Bending forward, he dropped his head into his hands and groaned like a wounded animal.

Cassie's heart ripped at the tormented sound, and she sped across the room to kneel beside him and place her hand on his arm. Everything about him stilled.

A moment later, he was beside her on the carpet, his arms around her, cradling her head to his chest.

'Cassie, forgive me.' Rocking her gently, he repeated his plea, giving her no chance to answer. Last night she'd vowed to keep distance between them, learn to live without his touch. Her resolve hadn't lessened, but oh, it felt so good in his embrace.

His anger shattered by her reaction, Jack was left drained and racked with guilt. The one thing holding him together was having Cassie nestled to his heart, her soft fingers touching his arm and her unique aroma calming him with every intake of breath.

He'd broken his sworn oath and lost his temper, after nine years of rigid constraint. The thought of losing her, of not knowing why, had smashed the restraint on his emotions. Letting *his* fear out as a tirade had frightened *her*.

He steeled himself and stood, lifting her with him. Grateful that she didn't pull away, he cupped and raised her chin, relishing the softness of her skin. Her face was still pale and he didn't deserve the compassion in her tender eyes. He ran trembling fingers over her cheek, stroked her tempting lips with his thumb. Ached to crush her to his heart and never let go.

'I had—obviously still have—a temper. I believed I'd conquered it. Instead, as we've both found out, it was just lying dormant.'

Her eyes widened, so big, so beautiful, and he struggled to contain the riotous emotions raging through his mind and body. Taking her hand, he led her to a brightly patterned couch and, without letting go, sat and drew her down an arm's length away.

Huffed all the air from his lungs, refilled them then made eye contact with her and held it.

'There was a girl. We were both nineteen, both proud and obstinate. She flirted and I liked the attention I got from other women.'

The accusations they'd traded had been childish, worded for maximum insult. The making-up had always been hot and heavy, the best part of their relationship.

'It was my fault she died. I walked out of the room in the middle of a volatile slanging match, and slammed the bathroom door behind me. She stormed off and went skiing alone on a run for experts only. One of the instructors found her crumpled against a tree later in the day.'

Cassie reached out and laid her free hand over his, her sympathetic gesture deepening the guilt for his churlish treatment of her. He'd never revealed the full truth of that day to anyone; now he felt cold and drained.

'That day I swore I'd never lose my temper again. Haven't until now.'

He'd ignored Cassie's request for privacy, and shown her his baser side. Accepting her right not to see him would have been the honourable course of action, however distressing for him. Taking hold of both her hands, he raised them to his lips and kissed each one.

'I'm sorry, Cassie. I shouldn't have come.'

He forced himself to bring both of them to their feet, wanting to beg her to let him stay. To tell him the truth about why they couldn't be together.

Stepping away, he kept touch, sliding his fingers down her arms and over her hands to her fingertips, keeping the connection as long as possible.

'I'd better leave.'

She nodded, a forlorn figure, arms loose at her sides, shoulders slumped, and…hell, he'd swear he'd seen tears forming in her eyes before she dropped her gaze. Nausea struck and bile rose in his throat, rendering him speechless.

Shame drove him, almost running to the door to prevent himself from reaching for her. If he held her again he'd kiss her. If he kissed her again he might never stop.

Standing between the two doors, he flung his head back, jaw clenched, body taut. Daren't turn around for fear he'd crack.

'I love you, Cassie. Nothing in heaven or earth will change how I feel. I'll never stop loving you.'

Closing each door with exaggerated care, he strode down the driveway, fighting tears that threatened for the first time since Bob's funeral. He'd let them fall then, a tribute to the mentor whose love and guidance he would always cherish.

Keys in hand, he stopped by his ute, leant his forehead against the door and thumped the roof with his fist. He'd never felt so low, so impotent. Cassie had stolen his heart, now it lay crushed in his rib cage, its beating sluggish, purely corporeal. If she didn't want him, he might, with effort and tenacity, accept what she said. But he couldn't because her eyes, her touch and her body belied her words.

He couldn't think straight, and his hands were shaking. Leaving the ute where it was, he strode towards the main road that led to the local shopping centre. If the fresh air didn't clear his head, strong coffee would.

He recalled every word she'd said, didn't buy it. She'd spouted clichés and used his background and business venture to hide the truth. Damned if he could figure what that might be.

Cassie heard the doors shut and pictured Jack striding away, spine rigid, features impassive and brain racing. Her own kept repeating his departing vow.

'I love you, Cassie. Nothing in heaven or earth will change how I feel.'

Heart-stopping words declared with deep conviction from an abraded throat. Jack Randell, property owner, and soon to be even richer, loved her. Desirable, connected and eligible, with a choice of any of the beautiful, privileged women in Australian society, his heart had chosen her.

With a jolt, she realised she'd wandered into the kitchen, where the kettle sat ready on the bench. A light ironic laugh escaped her. A nice cup of tea, the age-old standby for any upset or trauma. It was going to take more than a caddy full of teabags to ease her pain tonight. Or for a long, long time.

Hot mug in hand, she returned to her room and surveyed the jumbled bedclothes, where she'd been lying, her mind in turmoil. Tomorrow she'd explain why she'd been upset to the guys and Narelle. They'd hug her, say they were sorry, and promise their support.

She closed her eyes. For now, she'd...

Tremble? She was shaking from head to foot, the liquid in her mug slopping to the floor. With effort, she managed to set it on her bedside table before collapsing onto the crumpled sheets and curling into a ball.

Her heart throbbed with every hot tear that ran down her cheek, and she made no attempt to check them. She sobbed until her tear ducts were dry, her throat was raw and croaky and her ribs hurt from her shuddering breaths. Until, despite her conviction she'd be awake all night, the trauma of her encounter with Jack and insomnia from the night before took their toll and she fell into dreamless sleep.

She woke with a pounding headache, a damp pillow under her cheek and shivering from lying on top of her quilt. Her ceiling light stung her eyes and she covered them with her hands as she rolled off the bed.

Drinking the cold tea eased her dry throat. Her alarm clock read eleven forty-six, meaning she'd slept for over three hours. Her skin was cold and clammy, breathing was painful, and a bleak future loomed ahead. She swallowed two analgesic tablets, grabbed her towel from the rail on her door and headed for the bathroom.

The hot water was refreshing and helped clear the fog in her brain, leaving a troubling vision. Jack, his hands alternating between clenching and splaying, his chest heaving with agitation, and his eyes hauntingly shell-shocked.

Those were the fascinating green eyes that had shone with laughter, playfully enticed her out of her comfort zone and flared with passion as he'd made love to her. Now, in her mind's view, pain and disbelief dominated in their depths.

She'd convinced herself she'd only be a pleasant inter-lude in his life. Had she been devastatingly wrong?

Wrapped in her winter dressing gown, she accessed the photo she'd taken at the beach for the umpteenth time since that day. She loved his macho stance and, as she'd believed, his indulgent expression. This time, as she lightly traced his smiling image with her fingertip, she really looked with an open mind and heart.

A lump formed in her throat and tears fell unchecked as she saw the truth she'd never dared to dream. His eyes glowed with adoration. And they were focused directly at her.

He'd said he loved her. Jack didn't lie. Waves of longing rippled through her, tingles of warmth drove the chill from her skin, and her heart soared with hope.

Oh, Jack, I've been so stupid. You really do care for me and I rejected you without a valid explanation because of my childish fears. Will you…can you forgive me?

CHAPTER EIGHTEEN

JACK POUNDED ALONG the beach, his feet kicking up a spray
as the tide's ripples washed around his runners. A full day
after fleeing from Cassie's home, the pain was still un-
bearable. He avoided looking seawards, knowing the sun
was beginning to sink behind the clouds, sending a wash
of colours across the horizon. A picturesque backdrop that
Cassie would adore. She'd smile, her eyes would light up,
and he'd be unable to resist kissing her.

Hell, he'd found it nigh on impossible to resist her from
the moment she'd wriggled out from under his aunt's coffee table. He'd been a fool not to realise it was more than
physical attraction when a mere brush of flesh could jolt
him like a high-voltage terminal.

He loved her and refused to believe the passion she'd
shown in his bed was anything else than the ardour that had
consumed him. Her responses to his kisses and caresses had
made him feel more of a man than he ever had in his life.

Would she still be working for Mel? If so, maybe his
aunt's sympathetic nature would draw her into revealing
why she'd suddenly rejected him. Maybe...

He faced the truth. Whatever had spooked Cassie was
very real to her. The dogged tenacity people labelled him
with, tempered with patience, was his best chance of proving his love. When, *please fate make it soon*, she accepted
they were meant for each other, he'd be waiting.

Two long, hard runs on sand in twenty-one hours were
taking their toll as he turned off the beach. Last night he'd
changed into a tracksuit and runners in the garage as soon
as he'd arrived home at about ten. He'd turned his concen-

tration inward, blocking out everything but the swinging of his arms, the pounding of his legs and the *thump-squish* of his runners on wet sand.

Tonight, as he powered around the corner, sharp tingles skittled down his spine. He glanced left and right. Nothing. Trying to shake off the feeling, he slowed for the last few metres and activated his roller door.

On the way through the laundry, he dropped his T-shirt and tracksuit top onto the washing machine. Whether Cassie ever knew or not, she'd subtly changed him. He'd always keep his home neat and tidy; now it was also beginning to look lived in.

He went to the kitchen sink and swallowed two tall glasses of water. Shower first, nuke something from the freezer later.

His doorbell rang as he took the first stair, and his first instinct was to ignore it. Not a good idea if it was one of his cousins, come to check why he'd been abrupt on the phone to Val this afternoon.

Bracing for a cheer-up encounter, he opened the door. His breath whooshed from his lungs, his heart somersaulted, then took off like a speedboat, and he knew, absolutely knew for certain, he was wearing the soppiest smile ever.

Cassie, gorgeous, light of his life and possessor of his heart, stood on his doorstep, hands tightly gripping her handbag, white teeth biting the corner of her mouth and an anxious, pensive look in her beautiful walnut-brown eyes, big as saucers.

He couldn't fathom why she'd come, thanked every star in the sky that she had, and stood aside to let her in. It took effort not to touch her to ensure it wasn't a dream. Couldn't be. If it were, she'd be wrapped tight to his body, her eyes would be sparkling and her musical laugh would be zinging through him.

* * *

Cassie's feet were reluctant to obey his tacit invitation. Her brain commanded she stay and drink in the sight of Jack, dressed in track pants, sweat glistening from his naked muscled torso, until she was satiated.

She was breathless. His chest expanded easily. She was trembling. He appeared to be solid as a rock. Her frayed nerves were stretched to breaking point, and he was smiling as if…as if she were bringing his complete Christmas wish list.

'Cassie?' He only had to say her name and she was molten to the core. She'd spent the day imagining his every possible reaction to her appearance after her adamant statements last night. Most had been cordial at best; she'd even prepared for total rejection. Not once had she visualised his sharp intake of air, the fire flash in his green eyes, and his brilliant, welcoming smile.

Hugging her bag to her chest, she sidled past him, catching the tang of sandalwood, male sweat, and him. The slightest touch and she'd throw herself into his arms.

Every cell in her body was tuned to him as he followed at a socially respectable distance along the hall. The lounge looked as neat as always, except…the alpine painting was missing from the wall. Now she understood its significance.

Heart palpitating, she pivoted to face him, and found half a room distance between them. Framed in the doorway, he gazed at her as if he couldn't quite believe she was here.

'Cassie, I…' He cleared his throat and gestured at himself. 'I've been running. Give me five minutes to shower and change.'

She nodded, not sure where her voice had gone. She regretted his intention to cover up his magnificently honed torso, though it would definitely prove a distraction from serious discussion.

'Take a seat or you can make coffee if you like.' He gave

her a wry smile. 'Just don't disappear. I love you, Cassie Clarkson.'

His leaving coincided with her legs buckling at the repetition of his earlier declaration. Collapsing onto the sofa, she hugged herself, torn between joy and trepidation. She loved him, would forgive anything in his past. With eyes shut, she prayed he felt the same and could overlook the insecurities that had governed her actions.

She discarded her coat, paced the lounge while the coffee brewed, and rearranged the blue cushions. Put the steaming mugs on the coffee table and sat. Her stomach rumbled; she hadn't eaten since lunch, couldn't have kept anything, however light, down. Footsteps on the stairs shot her to her feet, spinning round.

Jack walked in and her world shrank to the space between them. He was the epitome of a Hollywood hero, dressed in navy chinos and a matching polo neck jumper. Everything she wanted, and more, from his damp dark hair to his bare toes.

Their eyes locked, and the desire his radiated sent hot tingles dancing over her skin. His lips curled in a captivating smile, and the yearning to have him close, body-hugging close, overrode reason as she willed him nearer.

Her heart blipped when he gestured to the settee and sat, leaving space between them. His slow caress of her cheek with tender fingertips sent her pulse soaring like a rocket launch.

'If I kiss you, I can't promise I'll be able to stop.' Rough, raw with emotion. 'I can't...don't want to fight the aching need to have you here with me every day, to hold you in my arms while I sleep, and wake to your sweet smile every morning.'

Butterflies beat frantically in her stomach, and her brain turned into liquid mush. He was echoing her greatest wish.

She was aware of her heart racing and her lips curling in an effort to emulate his smile.

His thumb brushed over her mouth, her lips parted and the tip of her tongue slipped out to taste his skin. He shuddered, sending a wave of satisfaction through her, followed by a warning signal in her head.

Reason clamoured for her to tell him now, hold nothing back before he kissed her. Before they both lost control. She took his hand in both of hers and lowered them to the cushion. He immediately covered them with his other.

Looking into his buffalo grass-green eyes that had captured her heart at first sight, she prayed he saw the love in hers. She squared her shoulders, took a quivering breath, and jumped right in.

'I'm illegitimate. Mum was my birth mother's sister.'

For Jack this moment instantly become one of his treasured memories—the moment she gave him her complete and utter trust, even if she didn't realise. It was an honour he would never endanger as long as he lived.

The blush on her cheeks accentuated the pallor of her skin. Her beautiful walnut-brown eyes held an enthralling mixture of uncertainty and hope. For him, her silent plea was as clear as if she'd spoken out loud.

Please believe in me.

His heart twisted. She'd been suffering the same pangs of despair he had. Lifting their joined hands, he closed the offending gap then laid them on his thigh.

He'd been prepared to beg, on his knees if he had to; he'd been prepared to accept friendship if that was all she'd offered. Then he'd have determined to resolve her perceived objection to their being together.

'I don't know who my father is and I have no idea if my birth mother is dead or alive. Her last short phone call was from Los Angeles fifteen years ago.'

Her husky whisper triggered the release of tension in

his muscles, replaced by elation that she was keeping nothing back. Drawing her close, he cradled her head on his shoulder, and grunted with satisfaction as she slid her arms around him. Bending his head to catch every word, he leant his cheek against her hair, relishing its silkiness on his skin.

'Tell me.' He kept his voice gentle and persuasive, and made soothing motions with his hands.

'She left me with her sister when I was two days old, and I only have a vague recollection of a lady who visited once or twice when I was young. My only feeling towards her is eternal gratitude that she gave me to Mum to raise.'

She paused, lost in a world Jack couldn't even imagine, then resumed, her voice more assured, strengthened with love.

'Mum was, and always will be, my mother, and I'll never regret a moment of my life—except for losing her too soon. All my memories are happy and of being loved unconditionally.'

A deep tremor racked her body, and his arms tightened. It hurt having no way to help except to be there. In future, he'd encourage her to tell him more about this special lady who had instilled so many redeeming qualities in the woman he loved.

She raised her head, her resolute expression telling him she had more to say. It came out in a rush.

'My parentage will impact on your family. I'm public school educated, don't know how to make small talk to strangers at parties or dress for elaborate occasions. I'll never have the social graces Mel, Val and the others are ingrained with; it can't be learnt. I'd be an embarrassment to you and your family. You should...'

Jack's jaw had dropped as she spoke, adrenaline stormed through him and he grabbed her by the shoulders, holding her at arm's length.

'You sent me away, were prepared never to see me again

because of a misguided belief you aren't good enough for us? Dammit, Cassie, that's crazy.'

She quivered under his fingers, her lips trembled and she blinked to hold back tears. And he, normally so macho and undaunted by danger, broke.

'Oh, Cassie, my love.'

He hauled her close and kissed her with all the pent-up hunger from four days and nights of not being able or allowed the pleasure. His hands stroked and caressed her back, her hips, her shoulders—anywhere they could reach. He couldn't get enough of her softness and warmth under his palms.

Her hands skimmed over his shoulders where they'd landed, over his collar and onto his skin, sending prickles of fire speeding down his spine. Her fingers teased into his hair, anchoring his head right where he wanted to stay. Her lips parted, his parted, and he...pulled away, chest heaving and every cell screaming rebellion.

He framed her beautiful stunned face, and dropped a brief kiss on the tip of her nose. Shaking his head from side to side, he searched for the right words, and felt them rasp his throat as he tried to explain why all she'd said made no difference to their future together.

Their future together.

It sounded good. It felt right.

'My precious, adorable Cassie. You captured my heart from the second I saw you, though I wasn't aware of how powerful an emotion you'd evoked. Now I love you even more for your courage, and your trust in me.'

Her eyes softened and she lifted her hands that had fallen to her sides and laid them, fingers splayed, on his chest, one over his rapidly beating heart.

'Temptress.' He groaned with need, had to resist long enough to make his final confession.

'When I carry you up those stairs, I want nothing hidden between us, my darling. Let me explain why I am who I am, then there'll be no more secrets.'

Cassie gazed into earnest green eyes shining with love and saw her future, bright and full of joy. She raised one of his hands from her cheek, twisted her head and kissed his palm. The tremors that racked his body echoed in hers.

'I feel like I've been released from shackles that bound me since Tara died. I'd rebelled against my parents and the career they chose for me. I'm ashamed of some of the things I did, the drinking and smoking. And there were always girls willing to date me and my friends because we had money and fast cars.

'Mel's home was my refuge, and Bob my confidant who kept me grounded with calm advice and no judgement. Away from them, it was as if I had no safety catch on my temper, and I would just let fly.'

He fell silent, and the bleak expression in his eyes confirmed he was remembering that fateful day. Cassie felt his heart hammering, and loved him even more for his vulnerable side, that he'd allowed her to see it. She hugged him harder, letting him know she understood.

'Tara was as selfish and hot-headed as me. Our fights grew more bitter and accusing. I was a jerk, she was a spoilt brat. There was no way we should have been together, and I'd intended to break up before the trip but she'd been looking forward to it.'

He stopped talking, shook his head as if to clear it then suddenly pushed upright and set her onto her feet.

'Let's go for a walk. Find some of that fresh brisk air you like so much.'

'Yes, please.' They'd share more details another day. Revealing long-held, deep-set feelings was emotionally draining. Cool, crisp spring air would be welcome and refreshing.

He helped her into her coat, picked up his keys and ushered her into the hall. Watching him shrug into his jacket, she felt a bubble of amusement rise in her throat and couldn't stop it from escaping.

'What?'

His endearing puzzled expression gave her a heart-warming vision of the future with a challenging child. Hopefully two or three. Or more. Pointing down, she managed to choke out a few words amid her glee.

'Intending to paddle?'

He stared at his bare feet as if he wasn't sure where his shoes and socks were, grinned and, in one smooth movement, swept her up into a long, deep, pulse-shattering kiss. She swayed when he let her go, bracing her hand on the wall for support.

'See what you do to me. Don't move.'

He took the stairs two at a time and came down almost as fast wearing sneakers but no socks. He stole a quick kiss, linked their fingers and opened the front door.

Stepping down to ground level, he turned to face her, features sombre, eyes twinkling in the porch light. He leaned in, close enough to kiss her, yet didn't. He was teasing. She swayed forward, frowned when he moved his head away.

'There seems to be a disparity in this relationship, Cassie Clarkson.' He tried to sound stern; she heard the underlying joy. 'I've declared my love for you a number of times. Don't recall hearing you say it.'

'Of course I have. I…' She hadn't. She'd thought the words so many times, told him in her mind and in her dreams. Been so stunned and then elated when he'd voiced them, she hadn't replied.

'I love you, Jack Randell. I'll love you with all my heart and soul for as long as I live.'

Flinging her arms around his neck, she pressed her lips

to his for as long as her breath allowed. Laughed with delight as he lifted her feet from the step.

'Hey, I want longer than that.' He swung her around and onto the ground. 'Until the next big bang won't be enough.'

Cassie wriggled in Jack's arms, smelt scented air and gum trees, and felt a light breeze. There was also a crackling sound she couldn't place, especially with a cover over her eyes. It was three days since their confessions and declarations of love, and they'd spent every possible moment together. Family and friends now knew they were together, and she'd been lovingly welcomed by everyone.

Yesterday Jack had been secretive, making phone calls in other rooms and kissing her senseless when she queried his motives. He'd kept her up late last night, and woken her early for a run on the beach. They'd hardly stopped for breath all morning then he'd told her they were going for a drive in the afternoon.

Soon after they'd stopped at Port Pirie for a snack, she'd fallen asleep wearing the eyeshade he'd thoughtfully brought along. The sun through the window and the soporific low drone of the engine had ensured she didn't wake.

Jack had flicked occasional glances across the cabin, and couldn't help smiling every time. His Cassie, his angel, features soft in repose. He loved her, his family loved her, and incredibly she loved him.

Pity she'd missed the beauty of the Flinders Ranges as they'd driven along the road parallel to the iconic hills with their unique bluish tinges. She'd see them on the return journey. This was a special trip to make her dream come true, and the cases and Esky he'd secretly packed were in the boot.

He'd detoured onto a track he'd travelled countless times, finally parking near a stream edged by native trees. He left the engine running, hoping it would prevent Cassie from waking too soon. The camp was set up, and the last rays of sun had disappeared before he gently roused her and lifted her from the now silent ute.

Placing her gently onto her feet, he drew her close and told her to keep her eyes closed as he covered her lips with his in a long, loving kiss. As he raised his head, he removed the eyeshade and stepped away.

'For you, my love.'

Her reaction was all he'd hoped for and more. Her hands clasped together at her throat, her lips parted in a joyful smile and her eyes grew wide, sparking with delight. His pulse soared and his heart pulsated with elation.

Cassie looked up at the bright yellow moon surrounded by a million stars in a satin-black sky. To the left where a light brown tent, big enough for two, had been set up. To the right where a shallow stream flowed between shrubs and eucalyptus trees. And to the front where two folding chairs stood beside a portable barbecue and a crackling wood fire surrounded by rocks.

'This is…' She was lost for words. 'Oh, Jack.' She threw herself into his arms and kissed him passionately. 'It's just like the image I see when you laugh, only better. It's magical.'

'I love you, Cassie. Love you and need you more than I can ever express in words.' His kiss was tender, reverent. 'Marry me, my darling. Have babies with me. Live, love and grow old with me.'

Joy exploded inside her like a New Year's Eve firework show.

'Yes. There's nothing I want more.'

With a whoop of delight, he swung her up and round then cradled her into his arms, tight against his chest. Wrapping her arms around his neck, she pressed hot kisses on his neck and chin.

'Nothing, my darling? I think barbecue dinner can wait. First I'll show you the pleasures of sleeping in the Outback.'

She laughed softly as he strode towards the tent, knowing that sleeping was the last activity they'd be sharing tonight.

* * * * *

If you enjoyed this story, don't miss
A BRIDE FOR THE BROODING BOSS
by Bella Bucannon, part of the 9 TO 5 miniseries.
Available now!

If you can't wait to read about another
gorgeous and wealthy hero,
then make sure to treat yourself to
HER NEW YORK BILLIONAIRE by Andrea Bolter.

MILLS & BOON®
Hardback – August 2017

ROMANCE

An Heir Made in the Marriage Bed	Anne Mather
The Prince's Stolen Virgin	Maisey Yates
Protecting His Defiant Innocent	Michelle Smart
Pregnant at Acosta's Demand	Maya Blake
The Secret He Must Claim	Chantelle Shaw
Carrying the Spaniard's Child	Jennie Lucas
A Ring for the Greek's Baby	Melanie Milburne
Bought for the Billionaire's Revenge	Clare Connelly
The Runaway Bride and the Billionaire	Kate Hardy
The Boss's Fake Fiancée	Susan Meier
The Millionaire's Redemption	Therese Beharrie
Captivated by the Enigmatic Tycoon	Bella Bucannon
Tempted by the Bridesmaid	Annie O'Neil
Claiming His Pregnant Princess	Annie O'Neil
A Miracle for the Baby Doctor	Meredith Webber
Stolen Kisses with Her Boss	Susan Carlisle
Encounter with a Commanding Officer	Charlotte Hawkes
Rebel Doc on Her Doorstep	Lucy Ryder
The CEO's Nanny Affair	Joss Wood
Tempted by the Wrong Twin	Rachel Bailey

MILLS & BOON®
Large Print – August 2017

ROMANCE

HISTORICAL

MEDICAL

MILLS & BOON®
Hardback – September 2017

ROMANCE

The Tycoon's Outrageous Proposal	Miranda Lee
Cipriani's Innocent Captive	Cathy Williams
Claiming His One-Night Baby	Michelle Smart
At the Ruthless Billionaire's Command	Carole Mortimer
Engaged for Her Enemy's Heir	Kate Hewitt
His Drakon Runaway Bride	Tara Pammi
The Throne He Must Take	Chantelle Shaw
The Italian's Virgin Acquisition	Michelle Conder
A Proposal from the Crown Prince	Jessica Gilmore
Sarah and the Secret Sheikh	Michelle Douglas
Conveniently Engaged to the Boss	Ellie Darkins
Her New York Billionaire	Andrea Bolter
The Doctor's Forbidden Temptation	Tina Beckett
From Passion to Pregnancy	Tina Beckett
The Midwife's Longed-For Baby	Caroline Anderson
One Night That Changed Her Life	Emily Forbes
The Prince's Cinderella Bride	Amalie Berlin
Bride for the Single Dad	Jennifer Taylor
A Family for the Billionaire	Dani Wade
Taking Home the Tycoon	Catherine Mann

MILLS & BOON®
Large Print – September 2017

ROMANCE

The Sheikh's Bought Wife	Sharon Kendrick
The Innocent's Shameful Secret	Sara Craven
The Magnate's Tempestuous Marriage	Miranda Lee
The Forced Bride of Alazar	Kate Hewitt
Bound by the Sultan's Baby	Carol Marinelli
Blackmailed Down the Aisle	Louise Fuller
Di Marcello's Secret Son	Rachael Thomas
Conveniently Wed to the Greek	Kandy Shepherd
His Shy Cinderella	Kate Hardy
Falling for the Rebel Princess	Ellie Darkins
Claimed by the Wealthy Magnate	Nina Milne

HISTORICAL

The Secret Marriage Pact	Georgie Lee
A Warriner to Protect Her	Virginia Heath
Claiming His Defiant Miss	Bronwyn Scott
Rumours at Court (Rumors at Court)	Blythe Gifford
The Duke's Unexpected Bride	Lara Temple

MEDICAL

Their Secret Royal Baby	Carol Marinelli
Her Hot Highland Doc	Annie O'Neil
His Pregnant Royal Bride	Amy Ruttan
Baby Surprise for the Doctor Prince	Robin Gianna
Resisting Her Army Doc Rival	Sue MacKay
A Month to Marry the Midwife	Fiona McArthur